ATEET – THE PAST

Raj Bansal

ATEET – THE PAST
Copyright © 2024 by Raj Bansal
ALL RIGHTS RESERVED

tecolandsfor@gmail.com or www.grbauthor.co.uk.

Publisher: Absolute Author Publishing House
Cover Designer: Rebeca @rebecacovers
Editor: Dr. Melissa Caudle

Library of Congress Catalogue-in-Publication Data
  Bansal, Raj

       p. cm.

Paperback ISBN, 979-8-89401-036-6
eBook ISBN, 979-8-89401-037-3

TABLE OF CONTENTS

Chapter 1: Satto Bibi

They were returning from Sunil's sister Sandali's *Rokka* ceremony, held at Sunil's ancestral home, high in the mountains in Northern India, in a small town named Kavli Jopa. The ceremony was grand and went well. Sunil's family was kind to Randhira for a change. Sandali's fiancée and his family seemed nice. Despite the long trip up into the remote wilderness and the mountains, the picturesque and stunning views during the day were a sight to behold. However, the beauty of the landscape took on a dark, sinister, and eerie appearance at night, especially when navigating the slippery, wet, winding roads with deep ditches on either side.

Sandali's fiancée's family left in good time. For them, it was a long drive back to where they came from. Randhira advised Sunil to leave early. Sunil said they needed to help clear up the house after the guests had left, stay for dinner, and spend time with Sunil's extended family, whom he did not get to meet often. Randhira, the practical, independent, strong-willed woman, gave in to emotion. They ended up leaving late, their emotions a turbulent mix of regret, exhaustion, and a lingering sense of unease. Randhira regretted this throughout the drive back in the dark. They had been driving for two hours already, and there were still three and a half hours to drive, their exhaustion becoming more palpable with each passing mile.

After a heated argument, they booked a guesthouse on Randhira's phone. Despite the tension, Randhira was determined to make the best of the situation. She read the reviews before she booked, and her heart was pounding with uncertainty. The most common comments she read about this guesthouse were in line. "Once you've stayed here, you wouldn't want to leave," which was reassuring. She ignored the one comment, "Do not stay here." She thought there was always one negative review for every place. There was another comment that she either misread or her arrogance ignored, "Once you've stayed here, you cannot go back." It was her arrogance, and she smirked because she had the opportunity to mock someone's poor English. Nevertheless, she booked Ateet for one night.

The recommended check-in time at Ateet Guest House was 10:00 p.m. It was 11:30 p.m. As the clock ticked past 11:30 p.m., Sunil's grip on the steering wheel tightened on his dark purple BMW. He could feel the tension radiating from Randhira, her gaze fixed on the darkness outside. The silence between them was heavy. Sunil had given up on trying to explain.

Ateet was an old, traditional, yet beautiful-looking guest house made of solid stone amidst snow-top mountains and valleys atop a hill near Lake Jopa. Despite the time, most, if not all, lamps, and lights were lit, and the backdrop of its surroundings looked magnificent at night. According to Sunil's car's satellite navigation system, they weren't far from it. Randhira ran her fingers through her medium-long black hair and huffed in disgust as Sunil clung tight to the steering wheel and manoeuvred through the tight, bendy, dangerous roads. He gathered the courage to speak in his deep, husky voice in an encouraging tone, "Only ten minutes more."

Randhira, still refusing to look at him, lifted a tight index finger in the air. She did not want to hear a word from his mouth. They reached Ateet, which was far more attractive than described on the booking site. Sunil parked the BMW near the lake, which glimmered in the moonlight. For the first time in the past forty-five minutes, Randhira looked ahead at the lake. She was still fuming.

"Shall we go in?" asked Sunil.

Her response was to open the door and violently step out of the car. The air was cold, crisp, yet clear. She breathed a decent amount of fresh air and walked fast and in anger towards the boot, nearly slipping on the wet, slippery path.

"Careful...the path is icy."

She raised her finger again, and Sunil stopped talking. She looked at him. Her beautiful green eyes and fair, gorgeous face were red in anger. Sunil stopped and stared. She looked ever so beautiful when she was angry.

She opened the boot, lifted her mini suitcase, put it on the ground, and walked towards the guest house. She knew they didn't have a fresh set of clothes for the next day, which infuriated her more. Slightly apprehensive of her surroundings, she bravely and angrily marched on towards her abode for the night. She experienced a strange feeling. Although the scenery was pretty, an obtuse sense of fear came with it. As she walked on, she got scared as she did, but soon relaxed when she heard Sunil's footsteps behind her and the unpleasant sound of the mini suitcase wheels running and scraping along the cold, hard ground.

She walked in first, put her hands together, blew air from her mouth into them, and rubbed them vigorously. Sunil stumbled in behind. At the entrance, Sunil and Randhira read the guest house motto, "*Ateeti Devo Bhava,*" which translates as "Guest is God."

"How original," mocked Randhira and headed towards the area that looked like the reception.

Ateet was traditional from the inside and outside. Stone walls, lanterns and lamps, old furniture, and curtains, wood-beamed ceilings, and an aging staircase surrounded it, but then there was a computer screen, a telephone, and a carpet. It was an old building with modern amenities.

Randhira liked what she saw, but no human was in sight until a couple walked out from a place that said, "Dining Room." Randhira saw a serious yet familiar-looking Indian man. He must have been in his mid-thirties, just like them, wearing a cream nightsuit. With him was a sombre Indian woman wearing a beige and brown nightsuit again, which Randhira assumed would have been his other half.

For the first time in three hours, Randhira looked at them and smiled. Sunil, too, looked over as he was looking at Randhira and did the same. The slim couple, still with a worried look on their faces, exchanged glances before reluctantly smiling back.

"Are they still serving dinner? Wow, it's late," Sunil said, loudly enough for them to hear him.

The male again reluctantly smiled and nodded, walking towards the old staircase. With Randhira and Sunil still looking on, they saw the female biting her lip. She gently pulled back the arm of the male, stopping him from walking on, and discreetly yet vigorously tilted her head towards the new guests. The male held her hand discreetly, yet vigorously, and shook his head at the female. His hunchback demeanor displayed that he was either frightened or just uncomfortable around people. The female pulled at his arm again. The male slumped his shoulders and strolled towards the reception and the guests. Randhira and Sunil were already bewildered by their behavior.

"Just arrived?" The man asked in a soft voice. Sunil nodded.

"I see," the man said, smiling, but his eyes did not.

The female tugged at his arm again. "Your house. Is it far from here?"

Sunil shook his head. "Just three hours away. We're tired and have been driving for a while."

"Oh! You might as well drive on," the male advised. The female pulled his cream nightsuit sleeve again, and the male held his hand to her and looked around.

"This is nice, but nothing is the same as home, right?" The female pushed the male out of the way and went closely up to Randhira and Sunil.

"If you can go, I suggest you leave for your home!" the woman said seriously under her breath.

Randhira and Sunil looked at one another, astounded.

"Jitni jaldi ho sake aap yahan se..." The woman was about to tell them to leave as quickly as possible in Hindi before she was loudly interrupted.

"Binki!" An old woman arrived through the door behind the reception.

"How are you, *mera bachcha*?"

The old woman went to the female and hugged her gently. *Bachcha* means child in Hindi.

"Was the food all right? It was your favorite tonight. You like Okra, don't you?" The old woman continued to talk, and Binki smiled, nodded, and looked down.

"Ajay," the old lady turned to the male. "Tomorrow, we'll make something you like, so it's fair," smiled the old lady. The male, Ajay, smiled and nodded, and he, too, looked at Randhira and Sunil.

"Don't go to sleep just yet. Wait for your food to digest," she spoke kindly and caring. Both kept their heads down, nodded, and walked towards the staircase.

"Binki..." she called out in a stern voice.

"*Ji?*" Binki turned around to look at her and obediently said, "Yes," in Hindi.

"Are you feeling well?"

"*Ji*."

"Shall I give you something, or will you be all right?"

"For what?" Randhira intervened, much to the old woman's disgust. The old lady immediately turned her frown into a smile as she turned her head towards her new female guest.

"She wasn't feeling well earlier. I gave her something for it, but it seems she still isn't feeling well," replied the old woman, turning back to Binki.

"No, no, I'm all right now. I don't need anything," Binki replied timidly.

"Sure? Because don't I think you're well," questioned the old woman.

"How do you know she is still not well?" Randhira interrupted again. "She just said she's all right."

The old woman closed her eyes, reopened them, recalled her smile, and turned towards Randhira.

"What can I do? I treat all my guests like my children. I have a mother's heart that always beats for her children. A mother is always worried and concerned."

Randhira smiled gently and unbelievingly, whereas Sunil's smile suggested her sweet words convinced him. There was an awkward silence. Binki turned around with Ajay, and they left for the staircase.

"Let's get you both checked in," the old woman said excitedly. Randhira and Sunil turned towards the reception. The old woman, dressed in an old-fashioned black sari with a golden border covering her head, walked behind the desk. Her forehead's big, circular, deep red vermilion was the most striking. It stood out like the sun.

Sunil began with his name, "My name is Sunil…"

"…Grewal. Sunil Grewal," called out the old lady.

Randhira and Sunil glanced at one another.

"Everyone else has checked in…only you remain…"

"Ah yes… sorry for that, we got…"

"…it's fine!" The old lady interrupted Sunil's explanation. "But generally, we like everyone to have checked in by ten p.m. We thought there may have been complications."

"Yes, there were…" Randhira began, only to be interrupted again.

"The Suite! Nice choice!" The old lady smiled. Randhira didn't like being interrupted, and it showed in her eyes.

"It doesn't say your name here, *beta*," the old woman said, turning to Randhira, who was calling her child in Hindi.

"Randhira…"

"…Randhira Grewal!" The old lady intersected her again.

"Bajaj!" Randhira corrected her intensely. The old woman looked at her with questioning eyes. Both women kept their sharp eyes upon each other.

"Are you not…?"

"We are!" Sunil broke in to answer the old lady. "Of course we are!" Randhira turned to Sunil in anger but, fortunately, kept mum.

"You see, Aunty…"

"Satto Bibi!" The old woman's voice was slightly elevated when she told Sunil her name.

"Everyone calls me Satto Bibi!" Again, she corrected with a raised voice. It was slightly too raised for Sunil and Randhira's liking.

"Bibi… *guesta naal eve gal karidi hundi ya?*" another person came through the door behind the reception desk. He asked Satto Bibi politely in Punjabi, "Is that the way to talk to guests?" He was a bald young Indian man with a thick black beard wearing a black kurta pajama. Satto Bibi gave him a stern stare as he came forward and stood next to her behind the desk.

The young bald man turned to Sunil and Randhira, "Sorry, Satto Bibi suffers from hypertension; sometimes she gets worked up."

"Porush!" Satto Bibi uttered his name.

"What, Bibi?" The young man asked Satto Bibi in his soft, soothing voice.

"Let me complete the check-in. So, Mr Grewal?" Satto Bibi returned to checking them in.

"You see…Satto Bibi," Sunil made sure he got it right, "We had a little argument on the way, so…"

"…Are you both married?" The interruptions were getting rather annoying.

"Yes…!" Sunil replied hesitantly as Randhira looked away in frustration. Satto Bibi noticed this.

"We are…married," Sunil continued. "She kept her surname after marriage."

"Anything to prove you are married?" the old lady interrogated. Randhira looked over at Satto Bibi in shock and horror. The two women would have been seriously injured if stares could have caused harm. Porush realized the guests' anguish and moved to defuse the situation, "Bibi, who these days carries around proof of marriage? Don't worry, Mr Grewal; it is fine."

"But…"

"…Bibi, in cities, women keep their surnames after marriage. It is all right," clarified Porush. The old woman continued with the check-in and extended the key to them. Randhira extended her arm to take it, but Satto Bibi protracted it towards Sunil. Randhira tightly clenched her hand into a fist the host left hanging mid-air. Sunil took the key swiftly and said, "Thank you."

"Top floor. The Suite," said Satto Bibi. Randhira and Satto Bibi's eyes were again at war for a few seconds before Randhira turned away. When Satto

Bibi saw Sunil take both cases, she got more flustered.

"The lifts are that way," explained Porush, pointing in the direction with his hands. Sunil nodded and moved in that direction. Randhira followed him. The couple went towards the lifts, pressed the button to call one, and waited for it to arrive.

"That woman!" spoke Randhira under her breath.

"Leave it, *yaar*," said Sunil, using the Hindi word for mate. "Remember, we are in the mountains. People are orthodox in these parts of the country. You know that. Don't you remember how Aunty Chhamo reacted when you answered her question?"

Randhira turned to Sunil, "Yes, she dropped her plate of *Rasmalai* when I said yes to her question, Are you both in a live-in relationship?"

"That *Rasmalai* was good," Sunil commiserated.

"It was her third plate! I did her a favor. Have you seen her size?"

Sunil smiled gently. Randhira, too, smiled back.

"Thank God you smiled."

"That doesn't mean you are forgiven," cleared Randhira.

Sunil smiled, and Randhira gently smiled and said softly, "I hate you."

"I know," Sunil replied with a bigger smile.

The lift arrived. It was big enough for both them and their cases. Sunil turned to the buttons. Instead of saying "first floor," "floor one," or "top floor," it just said, "The Suite," so Sunil pressed the button. This was odd because there were other rooms on this floor, too.

The lift took them straight up without stopping at any floor. The lift opened, and they didn't have to walk far to the Suite. The room was cozy, again, a fine mixture of traditional and modern. It had stone walls, a beamed ceiling, four-poster beds, old long curtains, old-fashioned curtain rails, and brass handles. Then there were menu cards, a telephone, a safe, drawers, and a wardrobe, a computer desk, electricity plugs, and a modern flat-screen television. The linin was fine white on Randhira threw herself and took a deep sigh of relaxation.

"I am so tired, Sunil," Randhira said as she stretched herself out, lying on her back, and closed her eyes. Sunil arranged the mini suitcases. After having done so, he threw himself sideways beside her and placed his hand gently on her fair navel, which was visible as her light blue rollneck jumper lifted slightly when she stretched. She smiled with her eyes closed. Sunil rubbed her bare tummy and moved his hand inside the jumper upwards. She smiled and laughed.

"No…" she said softly.

"Yes…" he gently replied.

She sat on the bed, removed her rollneck, lifted her eyebrows, and smirked at Sunil. She used the heel of one shoe to remove the other, then her toes to remove the second. She stood up, removed her dark blue denim jeans, and turned towards him.

"This is a new set," commented Sunil as he noticed her new lacy light blue lingerie. She leaned down to bring her face close to his, exposing her deep cleavage, and asked, "Do you like it?"

"I love it," replied Sunil, and they began to kiss. Sunil removed his cream rollneck and black jeans, and Radhira removed her jeans. They kissed and embraced each other passionately until they were abruptly interrupted by a loud knock on the door. Sunil turned towards the door while kissing her.

"Leave it, they will go," Randhira whispered, pulling him towards herself. Sunil ignored the knock, but the knocking got louder. Although angry, Randhira tried to keep a straight voice when she eventually asked, "Yes!? Who is it?"

"Satto Bibi!" A loud and strong voice came from the other side.

"What is it?" Randhira asked, again.

"Please, can you open the door? I brought you both mineral water bottles; you'll need them tonight."

Randhira slumped her head, rolled her eyes, and replied, "Yes, all right. Give us two minutes."

"Put your clothes on!" Randhira whispered to Sunil.

Sunil ran towards his jumper, which had traveled quite a distance within the room. Once putting on his jumper, he straightened his jeans. One of the legs was inside out. He eventually got them on and forgot completely about his messed-up hair.

Randhira grabbed her jeans, which were completely inside out. She first corrected them and put them on, then grabbed her rollneck and unknowingly put it back on inside out. She, too, forgot about her messed hair. Out of breath, both hurried towards the door to open it to pure elegance.

The short old woman stood there straight, wearing her prominent large red vermillion and her black sari, head covered, and quite surprisingly, with a large smile. She was holding two large, unopened bottles of mineral water.

"Hi," said Randhira as she opened it. The old lady's smile lessened as she saw them in that state and her jumper inside out.

"I bought you water," Satto Bibi said, handing them the bottles.

Randhira paused. She was not used to being looked after and was finding it difficult to take the water bottles and express gratitude.

Sunil came forward, took them, and said, "Thank you, Aunty."

"Satto Bibi!" This time, she shouted. Both Sunil and Randhira were taken aback by the host's contrasting kind behavior and offensive attitude.

Sooner or later, having gathered and processed that he had been shouted at, he said, "Yes, yes, sorry, Satto Bibi…Thank you for the bottles."

The old woman turned and said, "Goodnight!" Randhira quickly closed the door and leaned up against it. Both stood there bewildered and aghast.

"What was that?" Randhira said softly, pointing at the door with her thumb.

"I don't know, Renu." Sunil fondly called her Renu—he called her that- and so did her parents, a few close relatives, or one or two close friends. But most people did not know her by Renu. He, too, was dumbfounded by her behavior. Both stood there quietly for a second or two.

"Let's see this night out. We leave at the crack of dawn!" Randhira commanded softly and headed towards the bed. Sunil was still thinking as he put bottles on the desk near him.

"What was the guest saying downstairs before Satto Bibi interrupted her…?" asked Sunil. Randhira stopped and turned, her eyes enlarged when she remembered what Binki had said.

"Leave as soon as you can from here…" She replied. Randhira had a foul taste in her mouth after reciting Binki's comments. Sunil's eyes widened, too.

"And that's what we will do. Out first thing tomorrow. No need to say bye. We'll leave the keys at the desk and drive off."

Randhira nodded to Sunil's comment, but before he could add more to his words, there was another knock at the door. This time, both jumped at the knock, and their concerns began to turn to fear.

"Now what?" Randhira whispered to Sunil.

"I don't know!" Sunil, for the first time, shouted back under his breath. He saw Randhira was worried.

"Okay, okay, relax…I'll open it," said Sunil and courageously did so.

It was Satto Bibi again.

"May I come in?" she asked softly.

Sunil looked around, not knowing what to say, but ultimately mustered the courage to say, "Erm…we are very tired, Satto Bibi, and we would like to sleep if that's alright."

"I won't take much more of your time. This is necessary. I implore you."

Sunil blew out air from his mouth, gave in, and agreed. The short old lady walked in extremely slowly. She wore anklets with small bells, making a distinct sound as she stepped. Silence in the room made them sound more ominous and prominent. The old woman saw Randhira standing by the bedside table on one side of the bed with her hands behind her back. By this time, Sunil had closed the door and walked up to the end of the bed.

Satto Bibi first walked over to Sunil and tidied his hair with her soft old hands, which gave off a strange smell of burnt sandalwood. The old lady lovingly touched his cheek and said, "I am sorry, *beta*. We got off on the wrong foot. I didn't mean to shout, but I am traditional and old-fashioned. I like being called *Bibi*, *Biji*, or *Matai*, as all these words mean "Mother." Aunty seems distant and loveless."

Sunil smiled, nodded, and reciprocated her love by placing his hand on hers.

"That's fine, Satto Bibi, I understand. Our elders shout at us out of love and concern. Deep down, they want the best for us."

Satto Bibi smiled and said, "Mera *bachcha*..." She then turned to Randhira. "And you too, *beta*, I am sorry. Sometimes, my high BP gets the better of me."

"Has the doctor not given you tablets for that?" Randhira asked. Sunil angrily rolled his eyes at Randhira as Satto Bibi had her back to him. Satto Bibi's smile faded upon hearing that question. She paused, waiting for the question to digest and register with herself. She walked over to Randhira but placed her foot down harder at each step, so the anklet bells sounded louder.

"*Beta*..." she ran her hands through Randhira's hair, tidying it up, and continued, "of course, the doctor has given me them. But old people tend to forget. I may have forgotten to take them this morning."

Randhira nodded and became more afraid of the sound of the anklet bells and the burning smell emanating from her hands. Satto Bibi gently reached for her roll neck jumper and began taking it off her. Randhira did not stop her, although she was astonished at her action. Sunil, too, was in shock.

Randhira stood before her in a brand new, lacey, light blue bra. She was embarrassed. Randhira was a busty woman, and the bra displayed much cleavage. She covered herself with her arms. Meanwhile, Satto Bibi had straightened out the rollneck that was inside out, began to put it around her head, and eventually put the jumper back on her and tidied her hair again once it was on.

"We mustn't wear our clothes inside out," smiled Satto Bibi and placed her hands on her hips.

"You have strong hips. Child-bearing hips." Randhira stood there numb and stunned, not knowing what to do or say.

"Come…" said Satto Bibi. She put her arm around her and made her sit on the bed. Randhira quietly sat down with lowered eyes while Satto Bibi stood before her. She gently touched her cheek and said, "What I say is for your well-being, Renu."

Randhira looked straight up at her without blinking but didn't utter a word while despising the smell her hand was giving off. The burning smell; Randhira hated it.

"No more of... what they call it... having fun. You both must settle down, get married, and start a family," advised Satto Bibi.

"Satto Bibi, we are..." Randhira's voice was stifled.

"...Shush!" Satto Bibi gently placed her finger on Randhira's lips. "I know, you are not married," said Satto Bibi, putting her hand sideways upon Randhira's tummy and keeping it there, much to Randhira's discomfort.

"A boy," Satto Bibi said.

"Sorry?" Asked Randhira.

"The first child you will bear will be a boy." She took her hand away from Randhira's tummy and walked slowly towards the door, making sure her anklets made as much sound as they could, but before she opened the door and went out, she again turned around to the couple and said, "Be comfortable and sleep well. Tomorrow, I will call a priest, and he will get you both married."

Randhira's eyes widened, and her mouth dropped in fear, horror, and disbelief. Sunil's ears perked at the comment, and he amusedly looked at Satto Bibi. He noticed her conniving smile, laughed out loud, and spoke, "Satto Bibi, we have to leave early

24

tomorrow, but I promise as soon as we get back home, we'll get the marriage preparations underway and send you an invite. You will come, won't you?"

"No." She, too, laughed loudly and smiled back at Sunil. "You aren't leaving tomorrow morning because you are getting married … here…at Ateet."

Sunil didn't know what to say and smiled; then laughed again at what she had said.

"Please, Satto Bibi, stop joking with us." Now, Satto Bibi's smile had completely vanished.

"I am not," she replied assertively.

Sunil's tolerance levels were now being tested, and he, too, became serious. "We have to leave early tomorrow. As much as we appreciate your sweet gestures and kind, loving, and caring thoughts, we will decide our marriage date. We'll be leaving at the crack of dawn."

Satto Bibi paused and stared Sunil in the eyes. Sunil could see her holding back her urge to burst out in anger and display her wrath, which she hid immensely well and kept her assertive tone.

"That… we'll see," said the old woman.

"What does that mean?" Asked Sunil.

"Perhaps you didn't read what it said at the entrance of Ateet. *Ateeti Devo Bhava*! In case you modern people don't know, it means…"

"…We know what it means!" Randhira burst in.

"You do? Good! But along with that, there is another unwritten rule of this guest house… the guest comes here according to their will but only gets to leave when the host wishes them to or allows them to. Until we are not done serving you, you may not leave. We take extremely good care of our guests. They are loved. We take care of guests as if they were our children. So right now, you are Satto Bibi's guests, or should I say, my children and you will only leave when Satto Bibi says you can." Satto Bibi's assertive command was delivered with a confident smile.

"Again! We appreciate this, Satto Bibi! But we will have to leave! So, goodnight!" Sunil shouted.

"Sunil," Randhira tried to calm Sunil down.

"That *beta*… we will have to see…goodnight," said Satto Bibi, opening the door and leaving.

Sunil closed the door after she had gone, which left Randhira and Sunil frightened. They didn't say a word until they could no longer hear the anklets.

"Sunil…are you capable of driving now?" Asked Randhira.

"Yes, why?" Answered Sunil.

"Then let's leave now! I am getting scared."

"Are you crazy, Renu? She cannot stop us from leaving. We will stay here the night, go to bed now, and drive off at first light! Don't worry! I'll see how she won't let us leave!" Sunil was angry and adamant.

"No, Sunil…you didn't hear her."

"I heard everything she said!" Sunil was still shouting.

"Really?"

"Really."

"Then did you hear what she called me?"

Sunil was speechless and thought and eventually asked, "What?"

"Renu…she called me Renu."

Chapter 2: Car

Randhira was abruptly woken by the sound of the curtains being opened and the bright sunlight shining through. Half asleep, she checked her sheets. They were fully covering her. She liked to sleep in the nude, as did Sunil. The housekeeper was inside cleaning. Sunil remained undisturbed as he was still asleep. She made sure he, too, was covered.

Randhira slowly sat up. Anger and shock went through her mind. She could not fathom what the housekeeper was doing inside, who had not yet realized Randhira was awake. Randhira slid further up against the bedrest and noticed the young housekeeper.

The housekeeper realized one of her guests was up. "Good morning, Madam *Ji*!" she shouted in her sweet yet confident, chirpy voice, and continued to clean and tidy. Randhira, still dumbfounded by this all, held her head. It was heavy with a dull ache. The housekeeper's cheerful voice broke Sunil's slumber. He, too, covered himself with the sheet.

"What the! What!" He was about to shout when he saw the cleaner's innocent face and lowered his tone and voice. It was rather uncanny, but her resemblance to Randhira was one of the reasons he discontinued shouting.

"What is going on?"

The young cleaner put her hands on her waist.

"Sir, it is noon," she informed.

"What!?" Randhira and Sunil both yelled in unison and reached for their phones. The housekeeper was correct.

"We knocked, and knocked and knocked and…knocked," she said, smiling at them.

"My head!" Sunil exclaimed!

"Yeah, mine too," said Randhira.

"Oh dear, you drank all of it, didn't you?" Said the housekeeper.

"All of what?" asked Randhira.

"The water Satto Bibi gave you?" squeaked the bubbly housekeeper. They both stared at the bottle on their bedside tables. They were both empty.

"You see…" The housekeeper tip-toed up to them with an innocent yet cheeky smile and said, "She sometimes put a drop of something in there to help guests get a good night's rest. The guest normally drinks a sip or two or half the bottle. But you drank it all!" She began to laugh.

"This is ridiculous!" Randhira shouted, and the young housekeeper stopped laughing.

"I will deal with that, Satto Bibi! We have missed check-out time! Now they will charge us for another night!" Shouted Sunil. The housekeeper bobbed her head, unperturbed by their concern, seeming as though she was waiting to either smile, laugh, or crack her following chirpy comment or joke.

"Charge us? That's the least of my concerns! We are late; we should have been on our way ages ago," said Randhira. "We would have even reached by now! My Sunday is ruined!"

"Let's get up and get ready," Sunil said. The young housekeeper continued to clean.

"Please, can you leave for now and clean later? We only need another hour and a half to get ready, and then we'll go." The housekeeper bobbed her head with a faint smile, gathered her things, and skipped out.

The couple sat in the bed for a while in distress until they both got out and headed for their undergarments.

"How did she drug us? The bottles were sealed," Randhira said slowly and astonished.

"It's easy to tamper with seals these days," replied Sunil glumly.

"Renu…" Sunil spoke again after a pause.

"Yes…"

"Was it just me, or did that housekeeper look rather like you?" said Sunil bravely.

"Hah! Me! Seriously Sunil? You're telling me I look like a maid now! Fucking Ridiculous." Randhira swore little when she was truly angry, but she didn't look closely at the housekeeper. She threw the sheet off violently and stormed into the bathroom in a huff, naked. They took turns in the bathroom. While one got ready, the other packed. Both remained quiet throughout. Despite the awkward morning, the bathroom was modern, and the shower was amazing. Randhira loved it as much as she'd refused to admit that if asked. She didn't want to come out, as did Sunil when he showered. They felt clean and were ready to leave. Strangely enough, the shower calmed their moods and anger despite having to wear what they wore the day before.

It got to the point where they were ready to leave. Both checked the room to see if they'd left anything. They grabbed the key, took their suitcases, and exited the door and the room. In the corridor, the housekeeper was again working in another room. She smiled at them from a distance. Sunil and Randhira gave a guilty smile back.

"Goodbye," said Sunil.

"I will see you downstairs later," said the housekeeper with a big grin. She went into the room and out of their sight. Sunil chuckled at her words and looked at Randhira, who looked worried, and headed to the lift.

"Funny she should say that, right?" Sunil was looking for the same response from Randhira.

"I just want to go." Sunil knew she was worried, and in all honesty, so was he. The lift arrived, and the couple swiftly got in and pressed the button to take them down. However, the lift did not go all the way without stopping. It stopped at the floor below. The couple from yesterday evening was standing there. Both couples smiled at one another. Ajay and Binki entered slowly and turned their backs to Sunil and Randhira. The lift started going down, and the silence was deafening.

"Binki, right?" asked Randhira.

Binki looked over her shoulder and nodded.

"Randhira."

Binki, still looking over her shoulder, smiled.

Randhira saw Ajay take tight hold of Binki's hand, and as he did, she turned to face the lift.

"What did you say last night, Binki? That we should go from here?" Randhira blurted out.

Sunil turned to look at the woman.

Ajay pulled Binki's hand towards him. Binki did not reply and turned away from Randhira.

"Please say something," Randhira requested again, but before anything else could happen, the lift stopped at the next floor, and the doors opened. Porush stood there, waiting to get in.

"Good morning, my lovely guests!" He, too, was in a happy mood. He got in and stood before Ajay and Binki with his back to them.

The lift started again.

"Say Binki," Randhira said again.

This time, Binki turned her head toward Randhira, and her eyes spoke everything, imploring Randhira not to ask her anything. Porush did not turn around when he heard this, but he straightened his back and took a deep, heated breath through his nostrils. Loud enough for everyone to hear.

Randhira did not continue to ask anything else.

"I was saying the lunch is delicious here. It would be best if you had some," Binki said in her soft and stifled voice. Porush's shoulders relaxed, but he was still facing the front and standing straight. No more words were exchanged until the lift reached the ground floor. Porush did not turn around; instead, he stomped straight out of the main entrance with clenched fists, maintaining a posture that emanated nothing but heat and anger.

Ajay and Binki swiftly emerged from the lift and rapidly walked towards the dining room.

Randhira was finally downstairs, and that was all she cared about. She planned to put the key on the desk and advance straight through the main entrance to their car. No one was at the desk, so she took the keys from Sunil and placed them on the desk. Just as she was about to leave the keys and remove her hand, another hand appeared from behind and under the desk and solidly placed itself upon hers.

Randhira jumped at the sudden emergence of this hand and let out a loud shriek. Soon enough, she knew whose hand it was. Satto Bibi was behind the desk, sorting something out lower down behind the desk. She could not be seen because she was bending down. Randhira took her hand from between the keys and her hand hastily.

Satto Bibi smiled and asked, "Did you sleep well?"

Randhira and Sunil both looked disgusted. Sunil was shocked at her audacity in asking them if they slept well after putting something in their drinking water.

"Very well!" Sunil's answer was stern and slightly sarcastic.

Satto Bibi ignored his tone and further said, "Good! It's lunchtime."

"No, thank you, we'll leave now," answered Sunil.

"Go have some lunch," commanded Satto Bibi.

"No, thank you. We'll leave now. I understand we have overstayed and are late checking out, so we are happy to pay for the one night extra."

Satto Bibi laughed. "Go have some lunch," and looked down at the register.

Sunil and Randhira were stunned and peered at one another.

"Excuse me, we need to leave! So please process the payment!" Randhira was nearly yelling.

"Have lunch first, *beta*; we'll sort all that out later," Satto Bibi said calmly, slamming shut, closing the leather-covered register, and then looking expressionlessly at them, straight in the eyes.

"Fine! I have had enough," said Sunil, reaching for his wallet, taking out 15,000 Rupees, and placing them on the desk.

"We are leaving. Thank you and goodbye," said Sunil.

"I think you may have forgotten. You can only leave Ateet when we say you can," Satto Bibi replied with a wily grin.

Sunil turned to face her and paused before saying the following words, "We are going to walk out that entrance right now," exclaimed Sunil.

"Do you as wish. No matter what... you will return."

Sunil marched towards the entrance. Randhira followed him.

Satto Bibi smiled and let the couple do as they wished. Sunil stomped out first, and despite his fuming, he couldn't help feeling calmer after breathing fresh mountain air and seeing the tremendous scenery—it looked like a painting. Randhira followed him, but her only concern was to get in the car and drive away as quickly as possible.

Sunil walked up to the place where he had parked. Randhira was behind him but had eyes fixed on the ground as she walked.

"Where is it?!" shouted Sunil.

Randhira looked and ran up to Sunil.

"Sunil, where is our car?" She was about to burst into tears.

"*Yahin to thi*! It was right here! I parked it here! Argh!" Sunil had completely lost it. He ran around here and there like a madman pressing the unlock button on his car key, hoping to hear the double beep sound of it opening while avoiding slipping up many times before falling.

"Sunil!" Randhira screamed and ran up to him. "Are you okay?"

"Ouch! Yeah, I am; where is the car, Renu?" replied Sunil, getting from the icy ground. He brushed himself off and strongly ran his hands through his hair, nearly pulling them.

Randhira grabbed his face and made him look at her.

"I don't know what's going on. I don't know who took the car or where it went. Let's just go from here, Sunil," she said assertively and slowly.

"How, Renu? How? Are we going to walk? We are in the middle of nowhere!" Sunil was on the verge of breakdown.

"I don't care if we walk back! So, come on, and let's get moving."

"But our car, I am going back in and asking them!"

"No! It's most probably them. They have hidden it or taken it somewhere. They are trying to stop us from leaving. Don't you remember what that old woman said last night? But I will not give in, Sunil!" Randhira commanded.

Sunil closed his eyes and slumped his face further into Randhira's hands.

"Okay, let's go," he said.

They composed themselves, grabbed the mini suitcases, and started walking towards the path that joined the tight road.

As they walked away from the guest house, they saw Porush walking back toward them towards the guest house and greeted them pleasantly as though everything was perfectly normal.

"Mr Grewal! Ms Bajaj! How was your night? Did you sleep well? Have you taken Satto Bibi's leave?" he asked enthusiastically and with a significant smile.

"Our car is gone!" Sunil was angry.

"Car? What Car?" Asked Porush innocently.

"Our Car! My BMW!" Sunil shouted. "We drove here last night."

Porush looked around and then back at them and paused for a while.

"I see. Yes. You must have driven here. I mean, no one can walk this path. It is surrounded by a dense jungle that is filled with animals. No one could have walked here. They wouldn't have survived," informed Porush with a slight evil smile.

Sunil and Randhira looked baffled and irritated. Porush realized they were disturbed.

"Listen, it is cold here. Come inside, and let's have lunch and a hot cup of chai. I will make some phone calls and help you find your car."

"I am not going back in there!" Randhira interrupted and folded her arm, letting go of the mini suitcase.

"Why, Ms Bajaj? Did you not enjoy your stay with us? Ameeran, our housekeeper, told me you guys were sleeping until twelve," Porush said again, a slight glint in his eyes.

Sunil anger was at a tipping point.

"Listen, if you can help us, please do. Otherwise, we are going," said Sunil, starting to walk off.

"Okay, have a safe journey. But I must inform you of the animals," replied Porush as Sunil started to walk away, but stopped and turned when he heard that. Sunil and Randhira both had Porush's attention.

"You see, sir, madam…you are in the middle of nowhere. You will not find anything in either direction for at least two to three hours. No phone booth, service station, café, restaurant, house, or dwelling. That's why we chose this location so people can have somewhere safe. Before this guesthouse was opened, many travellers died on this road. Car or no car, if you get stuck on the narrow road, no one will find you and rescue you. There is no satellite signal on these roads. If your car broke down, you'd be waiting for days, if not weeks, before a human came. People plan these trips very carefully, sir. Once stuck, only the animals will get to you first."

"Stop trying to scare us. I am not scared!" Sunil said.

"Of course, we all say that. And I believe you… completely. I am not mocking you. Only trying to help you."

"You and your mother have helped enough."

"She not my mother." Porush corrected him with a stern voice and a strong look. Then followed a long silence as Sunil and Randhira looked here and there.

"Okay, you can go, sir. I won't stop you, but before you go, tell me one thing."

"What?" Asked Sunil.

"Tell me, what would you do if you encountered a bear?"

Sunil was answerless.

"Run? No, eventually, he will catch up with you. Lion? Tiger? Wolf? Can you outrun them? What do you have on you that would protect you against these animals? They are all around us in the jungle."

Randhira walked up to Sunil.

"How far are you from your home? Driving distance?"

"Three hours," Randhira spoke.

"Three hours! So, if you had to walk a distance of three hours, how long would that take you? So roughly 240km to walk. Say, for instance, you did not stop. The path was straight without any climb or descent, and you walked at the speed of between, say, four or five kilometres per hour; it will take you anywhere between fifty-five to sixty hours to get there. Give or take. There are twenty-four hours in a day. Do your math. You'll have to camp out there."

"I'm sure someone will drive by," Sunil spoke, grinding his teeth.

Porush smiled. "Up to you. Take the risk. Have a safe journey," said Porush.

He turned around and started walking toward the guest house, then started walking backwards and addressed them again, "Or you can just come back. Have lunch and a hot cup of tea, and I will make some phone calls to help locate your car," said Porush.

"Let's go. He's scaring us," Randhira uttered.

"But he is right, Renu," Sunil mentioned, slightly perturbed by his words.

"Listen to him!" Porush shouted so the couple could hear them. "Anyway, as far as I remember, those that have left by foot have never returned to their homes alive. With or without Satto Bibi's permission."

"Sunil! I am not staying here!"

"Then where shall we go? There is a jungle out there! He's right about the time and distance. Let's go back and have him make some phone calls. We'll be in the warmth and be safe."

"You make a phone call from your mobile now!" Shouted Randhira.

Sunil pulled it out from his pocket. "No signal, but I'll try calling someone. You check yours," Sunil advised Randhira. Randhira checked hers. There was no signal. Like Sunil, she called a number from it but had no luck.

Both, not knowing what to do and unable to think of any solutions, slowly started to go back to the guesthouse and dragged their mini suitcases behind them. As they re-entered, they saw Ajay and Binki coming out of the dining room. They saw Porush standing behind the desk with his head down. Satto Bibi was not in sight.

"Come, guys!" Porush said. "I will return in an hour, and we'll find your car. Have lunch. I'll come and see you in the dining room." He smiled and left before Sunil or Randhira could say anything.

Randhira and Sunil headed to the reception, and Ajay and Binki walked toward the old staircase. When their paths crossed, Ajay softly held Sunil's hand and said,

"I said, didn't I…You might as well drive on," he said softly, slowly, discreetly, and then started to walk up the staircase with Binki. Leaving Sunil and Randhira in the middle of the lobby, fear struck.

Before they could react, Satto Bibi walked up to them. The couple on the stairs stopped to listen.

"Told you that you'd be back," Satto Bibi said with a smile to Suil and Randhira.

She grabbed hold of Randhira's wrist.

"Ouch," shouted Randhira. Satto Bibi's grip was tight. Satto Bibi placed her two fingers upon her pulse and pressed down tightly.

Randhira struggled for freedom.

"Shush!" Satto Bibi shouted. Randhira let her listen to her pulse. After a while, Satto Bibi let go.

"There is time yet. You can get married today. I'll call for Bansi. I'll bring the bridal and groom's outfits to your room. Your room is the same. Your keys are still on the desk, along with your money," Satto Bibi said and turned to look at the other couple on the stairs.

"Take them to lunch," Satto Bibi ordered, then left.

Chapter 3: Sunil

Ajay and Binki saw Sunil and Randhira's plight and walked downstairs to them. *"Aye ye...*Come, let's get you guys some lunch. We've eaten, but we'll sit with you while you eat. After all, Satto Bibi said we'd have you ensure you've eaten."

"I am not hungry!" Randhira exclaimed.

Ajay smiled and said, "Well, you'll feel hungry at some point. Setting your eating habits according to this hotel's mealtimes is best. You won't be going anytime soon."

"You don't understand. We are going as soon as we find our car!" Sunil shouted in denial.

Ajay smiled again and said, "When you find it, that is. Let's go to lunch." Ajay turned and walked to the dining room. Binki gently took Randhira's hand and walked her into the dining room. Sunil took a deep sigh and followed.

"Why is she adamant to get us married?" asked Randhira.

"There must be a reason," replied Sunil.

"What reason could there be?" Randhira asked again.

"She checked your pulse, didn't she? She's waiting for the right time. Probably checking your cycle time," said Binki.

"I am not getting married," shouted Randhira.

All four kept quiet for a while. Binki clenched her fists and tightened her jaws, staring hard at Randhira, which everyone saw. A sudden change in nature shocked everyone. Ajay placed his hand upon her fist, and she relaxed.

"Let's rewind slightly," said Sunil, starting to reason. So, what intention does she have of keeping her guests here?"

"She doesn't keep just anyone, probably the unfortunate couples, especially those unmarried."

"Unfortunate! We are not unfortunate!" Exclaimed Sunil.

"Mr Grewal…Grewal? Yes?" Ajay confirmed.

"Yes!" Sunil shouted, rising from his seat.

"I mean to say she probably thinks she should now settle down."

"Were you unmarried when you came?"

"Hahahaha!" Ajay laughed. Sunil and Randhira saw a relaxing change to his body language and demeanor, which shocked Randhira.

"Sorry to laugh like that," Ajay said. "No, Mr Grewal, we are the fortunate ones. We are married. But you will be unfortunate if you don't proceed with this."

"You're not making sense. Perhaps she does not like people staying here out of wedlock," Sunil said.

Randhira looked horrified. Sunil just nodded.

"You should be happy! You're getting married. You love each other!" Proclaimed Ajay.

"You do love each other, don't you?" Asked Binki softly with concerned eyes.

Sunil's chest puffed up. "Yes! Very much!" He paused and looked at Randhira. Randhira's mouth started to ache as though she had canker sore, and her eyes were as wide as if she had seen a hideous demoness.

"We are in love, aren't we, Renu?" Sunil asked, grabbing her hand, and looking concerned, his eyes imploring her to say yes in front of this couple.

After a while, Randhira nodded and looked down.

Ajay and Binki glanced at each other with a slight grin.

"We thought so," said Binki softly.

"But…" Randhira spoke.

"But what?" Asked Ajay.

"Not just yet, not now, not like this!" She shouted, letting go of Sunil's hand.

"Not now… I can understand. Not like this… I can understand. But not just yet? I do not, Renu. How long do you want to wait?" Sunil asked.

Ajay crossed his arms and smiled. Binki folded hers, too, but she looked at Randhira in disgust. Randhira looked at everyone.

"I am not ready!" Randhira shouted.

"Not ready yet, or not ready at all?" Asked Binki. Although her volume was low, her tone was stern.

"What is that supposed to mean?" Randhira asked.

Ajay raised his hands in denial and said, "Nothing, Ms...?"

"Bajaj! It's fucking Bajaj! And yes, I will keep my surname if I get married!" Randhira shouted.

"Renu!" Sunil was shocked.

"I can't believe you are letting them talk to us like this!" Randhira shouted at Sunil.

"I can't believe you are saying what you're saying," replied Sunil.

"Why are you saying? You don't want to get married to Mr Grewal, Ms Bajaj, if I may ask?" Ajay asked.

Randhira placed both hands down on the table and leaned forward toward Ajay.

"This is my life!" Randhira ground the words through her clenched teeth. "I will decide what to do when. No one dictates my life. I will decide when I marry!"

"Of course! You seem like the woman who makes decisions, which I am not saying is bad. Every woman should be allowed to make her own decisions," Ajay answered.

"Then why is there a gibe in your tone?" Asked Randhira.

"No, I was just wondering. You are a beautiful woman, Ms Bajaj. Are you scared of marriage?" Ajay asked.

"Why would I be?" Randhira asked.

"Just… curiosity," Ajay said and smiled.

"Ever turned down someone before?" Binki said, looking elsewhere."

Randhira's eyes were red. Again, she slowly ground her teeth in anger and fear and eventually said, "No."

"That's good because it would hurt to be turned down, won't it, Mr. Grewal?" Binki asked Sunil.

Before Sunil could answer, Randhira said, "I haven't turned him down!"

Sunil didn't know whether to be relieved or worried.

The ruckus was ended by the sweet housekeeper, who bounced in carrying a large pot of *Daal*.

"Lunch is here! It is *Kali Daal*. A black lentil dish. A north Indian favorite." She hopped over to them and put it down on the table.

"I'll get the other things to go with it."

"Enjoy lunch, you two," said Ajay, walking out of the room, and Binki followed.

Sunil and Randhira were left alone in the room with the pungent smell of *Daal*. Eventually, the girl who resembled Randhira served all the dishes, and in pin-drop silence, the couple ate the food. After they finished the food. Sunil went up to the reception desk. This time, Satto Bibi was standing there.

"I need to speak with Porush," said Sunil.

"He has phoned the police station to inform them of your car," said Satto Bibi, trying not to look at him.

"I need to speak with him. I need a report," Sunil said firmly.

Satto Bibi glanced at him and then at the bridal and groom's outfits on the desk to the side.

"He's in the gallery. Go down to the left and bear right," she answered.

"Thank you," Sunil said as he turned from the desk.

"Take these!" Satto Bibi shouted. "Your outfits for this evening."

"We are not getting married!" Randhira said.

"Oh yes, you are, madam. No couples are allowed to stay here out of wedlock! I allowed one day, but not more!"

Satto came from behind the desk, took the outfits, and shoved them into Randhira's hands.

Randhira was bemused. The power in Satto Bibi's voice, the heat from her breath, and the fire in her eyes refrained Randhira from saying again. Sunil did not react. Deep inside, he was happy to see Randhira take the clothes, as he was becoming uncertain whether Randhira would marry him if he asked or not.

Sunil and Randhira walked over to the gallery. Porush stood before a portrait of a young man, perhaps even a teenager. The man in the painting resembled Porush, but he had hair and no beard.

"Porush," Sunil called him.

Porush wiped a tear from his eye as he realized Sunil was behind him and Randhira was walking up to him. Sunil acknowledged the painting. Randhira was still far behind and had not yet seen it.

"Nice painting," said Sunil.

"Of course. My brother," Porush said.

"Ah, yes! I can see the..."

"...How can I help you?" Porush interrupted, wiping the other tear from his other eye with a lump in his throat.

"My car. Did you report it?"

"Yes! The police know and are looking."

Randhira walked up to them. She did not take notice of the painting.

"And we are meant to believe you?" She asked Porush.

"Yes, Ms…"

"…Bajaj!" Randhira was angry.

"Yes, yes, my mistake. Bajaj. Ms Bajaj, it's about time you started trusting and believing people around here. So far, you have not been very good at that," said Porush, turning his face towards the painting.

"What do you…" Randhira saw the painting. Her face fell, her eyes showed dread, and her body began to tremble, but she composed herself before Sunil saw her, and she finished her sentence, "…You mean by that? I don't like your tone."

"I don't mean anything by it, Ms Bajaj. I will call the police station tomorrow and ask if they can fax it. Is that all right?"

Sunil nodded and said, "I guess so."

A velvet drape hung from the top of the painting toward the back of it. Porush, as slowly as he could, took the drape from the back and brought it to the front to cover the painting with it. He then turned and looked straight into Randhira's hardened eyes.

"Why cover it?" asked Sunil.

"It's our custom, Mr. Grewal. We put up pictures of those members of our family who have passed, but instead of placing a garland over it, we tend to cover it with a velvet cloth. Occasionally, when we wish to remember them, we lift the cloth and stand before their photograph or painting."

"Passed? Do you mean passed away? I am so sorry, Porush," Sunil sincerely gave his condolences.

Porush looked at Randhira, who was still stunned.

"Ms Bajaj, where are your manners?" Porush asked.

"I... I am sorry for your loss," Randhira said and looked away.

"Thank you, Ms Bajaj."

"Randhira nodded.

"Thank you," Porush replied, reciprocating Sunil's kindness with a genuine smile and nod. Sunil had seen other paintings like this.

"And they are?"

Porush smiled and brought a happier tone to his voice. "Some other time, Mr Grewal. Right now, you both must get ready for your big evening. Your marriage! I will send Ameeran everything else you need to get ready. For both the bride and the groom," Porush spoke and started walking off.

"I am not getting married!" Randhira shouted.

"Then I'm afraid you cannot stay the night," Porush turned around.

"What?" Asked Sunil. You asked us to come to stay and warn us about the animals and dangers of traveling at night, and now you ask us to leave?"

"I am saying that Satto Bibi and her husband will not let you stay out of wedlock. Satto Bibi's husband is a priest. He can get you married. Once you are married, then there is no problem. In any case, it's not up to me to decide. Satto Bibi decides."

Sunil and Randhira looked at each other bewildered. Porush left them in the gallery to talk among themselves.

"Sunil, let's go. I want to go. I will walk. I will camp. I will take that risk. There will be a car or something along the way! But I want to go! I want to go!"

Sunil turned to her in amazement and said, "Why are you so adamant about leaving? You'd risk our lives there but cannot proceed with a ceremony just to stay here?"

"Sunil, what are you talking about? Are you mad? It's not just any ceremony. It's marriage. How can we get married?"

"Aren't we getting married anyway, at some point?"

"Yes...but not like this."

"I know that, but let's just go ahead with it. And whom do you think will know? No one knows us here."

"That Ajay guy, I've seen him somewhere. At a party or business conference."

"Ajay! That buffoon? Your mind is going haywire. He was wearing a simple kurta pajama. The one you buy from the streets. He would have been in some good clothes if he were high profile."

Randhira flapped in frustration.

"No one will know we're married. In any case, you plan to marry me, don't you, Renu?"

"Yes... but..."

"But what?"

"It's early!"

"Early? I am thirty-eight, you are thirty-six!"

"Shut up, Sunil! Now you're being rude."

"No, you are being rude! And I am beginning to think that you don't have any intention of getting married to me.

"Sunil! How can you say that? I love you!"

"Then prove it!"

"By getting married to you today. How old fucking fashioned is that. What a dumb thing to say!"

"Listen… I don't believe in this marriage, and neither do you; then, let's just fucking go ahead with it for the sake of things and our situation. We are stuck here! For us to stay, they want us married. We get married!"

"No… I can't, Sunil."

Sunil took a deep breath.

"Renu, I am going upstairs and getting ready!"

"This is their trap and conspiracy!"

"What trap? What conspiracy! To get us married. Are you hiding something from me?"

61

"No!"

"You are!"

"Sunil!"

"Then why did you say conspiracy or trap?"

"Like they trapped Ajay and Binki. They trap all couples like us and get them married!"

"At first, I thought that, but Ajay and Binki's changed behavior at lunch seemed as though they were comfortable here," Sunil replied.

"They are getting their guests married off!" Randhira shouted.

"Now I'm beginning to think they are doing a good deed!"

"Oh, shut up, Sunil."

"Renu, I am going upstairs and getting ready. And I say you'd better do the same!" Sunil commanded and stomped towards the lifts, taking his outfit from her.

"What's gotten into you, Sunil?" Randhira asked as he walked off silently without giving a reply.

Chapter 4: Aaroush

Randhira flapped, jerked angrily in the gallery, and marched towards the reception desk. "Satto Bibi!" Randhira shouted. No one came to the call. "Satto Bibi!" Randhira yelled again.

Randhira walked around the lobby and heard the slow movement of anklet bells walking towards her. The bells' sounds became prominent and stopped behind her.

"Shouting again, Renu?" asked Satto Bibi.

Randhira turned around.

"Look, enough of the façade! What do you want? Who are you, and why have you kept us here!?" shouted Randhira.

"*Chup kar*! *Holi bol*!" Satto Bibi told Randhira to keep quiet twice, first in Hindi and then Punjabi, but her voice had elevated to the heavens. Much louder, fiercer, and scarier than Randhira's.

"Just go upstairs and get ready, you arrogant girl," commanded Satto Bibi.

"How dare you speak to me like that, you old woman!" Randhira gathered the courage to shout back.

"Oh, shut up, you stupid girl! ... Just go upstairs and get ready. I need to set up the *mandap* for your marriage. I have lots to do! Don't give me a headache," Satto Bibi yelled.

"I am not getting married," Randhira confirmed.

"Go tell your boyfriend that! It wouldn't be the first time you are telling someone this!" Satto Bibi shouted.

"What do you mean by this?" Randhira had tears of fear in her eyes.

"Bibi!" Porush entered the lobby, where the two women were having words. "You can't speak to the guests like this."

"Oh, leave it! Guests, my foot! You have kept us here for a reason. This is a conspiracy. I will make calls, send emails, and post on social media, and someone will come and rescue us."

"Ms Bajaj, I assure you, you have nothing to be worried about. Please relax, go upstairs, and get ready. Tonight's your big night," smiled Porush.

"Shut up! I am not getting married!" Screamed Randhira. "I will go upstairs and make some calls!" She barged through the two, pushing Satto Bibi and Porush out of the way.

"We would like to inform you that the entire network of this area is down. The telephone lines are jammed. Please accept our sincerest apologies for this lack of service," said Porush.

Randhira stopped, turned towards them, and checked her phone. She saw the telephone at the reception. She went up to it. She lifted it. It had no dial tone.

"You can try your phone, but haven't you already tried that outside?" smirked Porush.

"I will not let you succeed in your endeavours, whatever they may be. I get to the bottom of this.

This is a conspiracy against me! When my daddy finds out about this, he will…" Randhira.

"…Kill us?" Finished Porush. "Why not? The rich and famous Mr Ganpat Bajaj can have anyone, shall we say 'removed' whenever it suits him."

Randhira kept silent.

"When you lose someone close to you to Ms Bajaj, a little bit of you dies along with them. I have lost three members. We all are half dead anyway. How much more can you kill us?"

"I am not getting trapped in your words or wisdom!" Yelled Randhira.

"Thanks to God, you at least saw some wisdom in them. Now do as Satto Bibi says, or else…"

"…Or else what?" asked Randhira.

"…Or else…leave Ateet! And take that boyfriend of yours with you!"

"Fine! I will! I don't want to stay in your stupid guest house any longer! This Ateet can go to hell."

"Ateet… The meaning of Ateet is the past!" Satto shouted.

"I am aware!" Randhira shouted back.

"And our past never goes to hell, Ms Bajaj! It always finds a way of coming back!" Exclaimed Porush.

Randhira saw hard into Porush's eyes. Both looked deep into each other's eyes, now red with anger.

Randhira turned around and started to walk towards the lifts.

"Oh yes, when you leave and bump into a wolf or lion, ensure you get your selfie with them. When you travel nearer to the city and get a signal, post it on your social media!" jeered Porush.

"Argh!" Randhira screamed, stomped her foot, and pressed the button hard more than once.

"This girl is mad!" Satto Bibi shouted so that Randhira could hear.

"Shut up! Just Shut... Up!" Randhira screamed back and got into the lift when it arrived.

When it closed, Randhira broke into tears and sobbed hard in the lift. The lift took her to the Suite. She stomped out of the room and knocked hard on the door. Sunil was surprisingly getting ready for his marriage in his white T-shirt and designer pajama bottoms. He opened the door and saw Randhira's numb eyes, and she sprung her arms around his neck and began to sob more.

Sunil was baffled by this behavior and asked her, "What happened?"

"That Porush, that Satto Bibi, threatened me!"

"Of what?" Sunil was angry.

"That if I don't get married to you then…"

"…Then?"

"…They will ask us to leave!"

Sunil's tense shoulder slumped, and he replied, "She has told us this before."

Randhira threw the red bridal sari on the bed hard, sat on the end of it, and began to cry.

"Look, Renu… Please don't cry," Sunil pacified her.

"I want to go from here, Sunil!" Randhira shouted.

"We are in the middle of nowhere!"

"Are you in on this as well, Sunil?" Randhira asked stupidly.

"What rubbish! You booked this hotel, Renu. "In on this!" So, you reckon I am tricking you into getting married to me? Trust me, Renu, I won't go this far and conspire against you."

"What am I going to do?"

"Go shower and get ready…we're getting married."

She punched the bed pillow and stormed into the bathroom. Sunil heard the shower turn on. Luckily, while she was in the shower, Ameeran came to the room and handed Sunil, the bridegroom, complimentary accessories, and necessary ornaments for the wedding. Downstairs, the altar, or the mandap was set up beautifully for the couple. Satto Bibi and Porush set it up like they would for one of their kin. A large meeting room was chosen for the wedding. The room was decked with fresh flowers and smelt of roses, sandalwood, and saffron. The sight was delightful. The priest, Satto Bibi's husband, Bansi, wore his best outfit and prepared all the necessary *havan* accessories, and everything looked terrific.

The couple upstairs looked delightful, too. The groom looked like a demigod, and the bride looked like a celestial woman who had descended from heaven. She looked divine.

They both quietly got into the lift and went down to reception.

When the lift opened, they found Ajay and Binki standing there. Binki looked completely different in her expensive royal blue sari with a silver border and matching silver trinkets. She looked magnificent. Meanwhile, Ajay stood beside her in his designer Sherwani, wearing a pink turban. He, too, looked like a prince.

Both smiled. Binki softly took hold of Randhira's arm, and Ajay put his arm around Sunil's shoulder and began to walk them to the meeting room. Randhira kept looking at Ajay in his new avatar. She was now sure she had seen him somewhere.

The couple walked into the room and was completely awed by the décor. It was as though they had walked through the gate of paradise. Porush looked amazingly different. He wore a cream kurta pyjama. Satto Bibi stood in an expensive, elegant white and cream sari. Porush came forward, took Sunil, and sat him down at the altar. Satto Bibi did the same to Randhira. Ajay, Binki, Porush, and Satto Bibi sat around the altar, and their eyes were set on the priest to begin proceedings.

Randhira's heart raced. Sweat droplets dripped down her face, taking along some of the bridal makeup. Her mouth felt as though she had bit hard on a bitter gourd. The silence was deafening. Sunil's shoulders were relaxed. Although baffled by everything, he was happy he was marrying his life's love.

Bansi began the mantras and rituals. The varmala was exchanged, and the rituals reached the point where the couple circled the holy fire. Sunil and Randhira both got up. Sunil was to step toward first, and as he did, he felt a tug, as though someone had pulled him back. Randhira had untied the knot between her and Sunil's chunni, which was bound during the rituals by Satto Bibi, before they had to walk around the fire. Randhira pulled from her neck the flower garland, the varmala, so hard it fell off her, and the flowers scattered everywhere.

Sunil's was left standing in devastation. She walked around the altar, and everyone sitting down got up. She went and stood at a distance from the altar and faced everyone.

"I can't do this! I just can't."

"So...you won't marry me...ever?" Asked Sunil.

Randhira shook her head, began to cry, and said, "No!"

Satto Bibi and Porush looked at one another and nodded.

"Ever?!" Screamed Sunil.

"No!" Randhira answered back under her breath.

"Then why are you with me? Is this just a big joke for you?!" Asked Sunil.

"No...I love you, but I don't want to get married," she explained.

"Why? And when were you planning on telling me this?"

"I cannot explain why, but I cannot. And I just wanted to see how things went and just wanted to carry on like this," spoke Randhira.

"Oh! Oh, my dear God! You have played me, Renu," Sunil spoke, and he, too, had now had tears in his eyes.

"No, I love you. Out of everyone I had a relationship with, I have loved you the most! I have not hidden anything from you about my past relationships."

"Yes! She has told you everything, Sunil… haven't you, Renu?" Satto began to walk over to them. Randhira hated the sound of her anklet bells.

"What does that mean?" asked a disheartened Sunil.

"I don't know what to say…" said Randhira, sobbing.

"We knew she was not going to go ahead with this. Do you now see the light and what is in his girl's heart, Mr Grewal," Porush said, walking up next to Satto Bibi.

Sunil's head went dazed, and he began to lose his balance. His body went numb upon hearing that the love of his life would not marry him. He removed his headgear and threw it in the fire. Everyone jumped away from the blazing flames, the heat it generated followed by the smoke as the fire went out. Bansi stood up, put his hands behind his back, and began to walk away without saying anything.

"I am leaving this place," Sunil turned to Satto Bibi and Porush. His state of mind was punctured. He was gutted.

"Mr Grewal, we have another room for you tonight. Rest there. We won't let you leave now," Porush said sympathetically. "We'll all talk in the morning. As for you, Ms Bajaj, you know where the Suite is." Again, Porush spoke politely and put his hand on Sunil's shoulder.

"I think it has been a long day for all of us. Let's all get some sleep, and we'll speak tomorrow," Satto Bibi said, walking up to Sunil and putting a caring hand on his back. Sunil withdrew from Porush and Satto Bibi and began to walk toward the meeting room door, and on his way past Randhira, he spoke the word,

"I don't want to see you again, ever in my life!" Sunil spoke the words and brushed past her. Leaving her with her head lowered and sobbing even more. Sunil continued weeping quietly as he stumbled, and he made his way like an intoxicated, motiveless madman.

"Porush, stop him. Don't let Sunil go outside during the evening… he will be about. Sunil's life is in danger," said Satto Bibi, with a straight.

"What? Sunil's life is in danger. How?" Randhira asked, realizing what she had heard.

Porush marched ahead to stop Sunil and turned his head toward Randhira as he walked past her. He said, "What do you care?"

Randhira, knowing Sunil was in danger, ran after Porush.

"Come with me," said Satto Bibi to Ajay and Binki. Satto Bibi walked in the direction of Sunil, Porush, and Randhira. Ajay and Binki timidly followed Satto Bibi.

Sunil had exited the hotel and was halfway up the path towards the main road. It was dark. The freezing wind was howling, but it smelt extremely fresh. Sunil was stopping for no one. Porush walked swiftly to catch up, whereas Randhira ran past him outside and grabbed Sunil's arm. Sunil shrugged it off violently.

"Let go! I felt betrayed! You hurt me!" Screamed Sunil as he sobbed.

"No, No, Sunil. I loved you with all my heart!" Randhira explained as she cried. The situation became hysterical and emotionally violent as the two tussled, and Sunil tried to free himself from Randhira's grasp.

"Come back, you both; it is not safe!" Porush shouted as he hurriedly approached them.

"Yes, Sunil, it is not safe out here. Satto Bibi said your life is in danger," Randhira said to Sunil in a teary voice.

"My life is over now. Enough of what Satto Bibi and Porush have to say. I am not staying here one second!"

Porush approached them and shouted at them both, "Your drama can continue inside. Right now, we must get inside before he comes!"

"Before whom comes?" Randhira asked.

Before Porush could reply, there was another in their presence.

Satto Bibi, Ajay, and Binki stood at Ateet's main entrance and looked up at the frightening sight.

Porush, Sunil, and Randhira all looked ahead. No one was in sight. The shadow of the trees darkened the part of the path where it was. The three heard the slow, stomach-wrenching, heart-stopping deep snarl. Shiny, bright eyes could now be seen as the figure moved slowly onto the path where the moonlight shone.

The shadow came close, and the snarl slowly turned into a growl. Although everyone recognized the snarling sound, the growl confirmed what it was.

Randhira's eyes enlarged in fright, and Sunil went pale with fear. In contrast, Porush pulled the two behind him and stood before them. He had an assertive concentration on his face and moved forward slowly to protect Sunil and Randhira from the creature.

The creature walked forward and came into sight. First, the large paws were seen, followed by the largemouth, jaws, and extremely sharp, bloodthirsty teeth. Deathly eyes, long whiskers, and a perfect mane were also seen. An enormous lion stood, moving toward Porush, Randhira, and Sunil, slowly snarling and growling.

"Stop!" Porush shouted at the large cat and raised his hand straight out in the air, palm facing the lion's face. The lion roared in anger. In a rage, he lifted his forelegs off the ground. As he did, he displayed his sharp, deadly claws, extending his jaw as wide as he could, striking terror in the eyes of his onlookers.

The lion moved forward slowly, snarling. For a while, it paused and looked at Randhira. The lion's eyes turned passionate from furious, but when he saw Sunil, the fury returned to his eyes, and he growled and moved in towards Sunil.

Porush guarded them both.

"Stop right there! Go back!" Porush shouted as loud as he could.

The lion threw a fit of temper and frenzy, snarling, growling, and roaring as though he was getting Porush to move out of his path. The lion raised its paws and acted as though telling Porush to move.

"No! No! Stop! Go Away!" Porush stood still as Sunil and Randhira moved back slowly when they could.

The lion's anger had reached its zenith, displaying a fiercer roar, hysteria, and agitation. Porush stayed where he was, with his hand out palm facing the lion, and did not move.

The lion leaned back and made a half leap towards Porush momentarily. Porush kept his stance. The lion's back legs were firmly on the ground, the abdomen low. The lion pretended to leap but lifted his front paws in the air and moved slightly towards Porush's face.

Seeing this, Porush lowered his hand and moved his face in, "Aaroush! No! Stop!"

The sight was beyond imagination, a man, and lion face to face. The lion was half in the air, paws up, and jaw wide open, and the man was facing completely towards the lion, his face full of anger.

The lion retracted, turned, and ran off.

Porush released his breath, and so did Sunil and Randhira.

Porush wiped the sweat from his face and turned toward Sunil and Randhira.

"Let us…go inside…we can talk…indoors," Porush was out of energy and breath. "I said…it is not safe out here at this time of the night."

Sunil could not feel his legs, and neither could Randhira. Both turned around slowly but looked backwards. Porush protected them and walked them toward the entrance, where Satto Bibi, Ajay, and Binki beheld nothing but a miracle.

Nothing was said until everyone re-entered the guest house, and Porush firmly shut and locked the main entrance.

"Ameeran!" Porush shouted as loud as he could.

Upon hearing her being called upon in such a way, the girl came before everyone fearfully.

"Yes," asked Ameeran.

"Go seal all other exits, doors, and windows?"

"All should be, but I will check again," she said the girl said and ran to the task.

"I will get water…for everyone," Porush said, still exhausted, and went to get what he said he would.

He returned with a jug and as many glasses as he could carry. He placed the glasses on the reception desk, filled them, and handed them to everyone. Ajay and Binki had to share, as there were not enough for everyone. All drank in fear and silence.

"Don't worry; he won't return," reassured Porush. "Mr Grewal, your room is now on the second floor. It's the first on the right as you exit the lift. I will get the key for you. Ms Bajaj, you can stay in the Suite," Porush continued.

"What just happened?" Sunil asked.

"Porush told you there are wild animals out here. It is not safe during the night," Satto Bibi spoke.

"No...no... the lion listened to you," Sunil said, pointing to Porush. Randhira, too, came forward and stood beside Sunil to confront Porush.

"Why did the lion listen to you?" Randhira asked.

Porush was still breathless, "Everyone...it has...been a long day, so I request you...let's talk tomorrow morning. I will explain everything. I'll bring the key, Mr Grewal," Porush said and began to walk away.

"You called it Aaroush," said Randhira.

"I am glad you realized, Ms Bajaj. Why? Does the name ring any bells?" Porush stopped and turned. "Yes, I called it Aaroush because that is his name."

"A lion named Aaroush? He's trained or domestic?" Sunil asked.

"Nor trained nor domestic. He is family." Porush's words stunned everyone.

Satto Bibi ambled towards Randhira, but the anklet bells could have been more conspicuous this time.

"Renu, our past, our Ateet, cannot be separated from our present or future. That's why we must always do the right thing, the past has a way of returning, so if we have done something good, it will return in the form of goodness. Whenever we do something bad or wrong, we feel, "Oh, it shall pass, or it will eventually go away," yes, you're right; it does for the time being. But when it does return, it returns with horrors."

Satto Bibi left the lobby. Ajay and Binki swiftly moved toward the stairs. They, too, were afraid. Sunil, astonished by what Satto Bibi said, turned away from Randhira and waited for Porush to bring him the keys to his new room. Randhira stood by until Porush did so.

Porush bought him the keys, and Sunil and Randhira silently took the lift to their floors. Ameeran helped take Sunil's things from the Suite to his new room. Everyone was in for a long, dark, frightening, sleepless, and lonely night.

Chapter 5: Porush

No one slept a wink that night. Ajay and Binki lay tight together, holding hands. Sunil and Randhira were alone in their respective rooms and kept awake all night. Everyone waited impatiently for sunrise so they could go downstairs and ask Porush and Satto Bibi about Aaroush, the lion. Sunil was the first to go down. He left the bed in his new room and went downstairs in pajamas.

After feeling dejected from the previous night's event, he was both emotionless and anxious. He found Bansi downstairs. Both exchanged stares, and Bansi walked off before Sunil could say anything.

Bansi was an old, hunchbacked, bald Indian man with a long gray beard. Like Satto Bibi, he wore black Indian clothes and walked with a thick wooden stick. He was a man of few words.

Sunil looked around and heard Satto Bibi's anklets. It was her.

"Up early?" She asked.

"I didn't sleep," replied Sunil.

"I didn't think so. How can anyone sleep with so many unanswered questions."

"Then answer them for me," Sunil said.

"The time is not right. You will be told everything in good time," Satto Bibi responded.

"How do you know her close ones call her Renu? I call her that. Or her parents. Maybe a few others," said Sunil.

"There was one other," Satto Bibi told.

"Whom?" Asked Sunil.

"In good time, Mr Grewal," Satto Bibi answered.

"If you say that one more time, my head is going to explode. No one here gives a straight answer; I need someone to tell me something before I go mad," said Sunil.

"I understand your predicament, Mr. Grewal, but that girl needs to learn, realize her mistakes, and take responsibility. We have waited so long for this moment, and now that she is here, we cannot let go of this opportunity,"

"Are you talking about Renu? What mistakes? Has she wronged you?"

"In good time, Mr Grewal," answered Satto Bibi.

"Tsk," Suni let out a deflated and disingenuous smirk. "Time...it seems we have all the time in the world, don't you?"

"Time is what we don't have, Mr Grewal. I understand your frustration, but it is best to wait sometimes," spoke Satto Bibi. "There... your head didn't explode now, did it?"

"But..."

"Porush will be here soon, and when everyone is here, then we shall all talk." There was a pause after Satto Bibi said that.

"Go to the dining room and have some breakfast. Ameeran has prepared the food," told Satto Bibi.

Sunil slouched, slowly took himself to the dining room, and began eating. Ajay and Binki, too, joined him shortly. Their eyes told their story. There was no sleep for them either. No words were exchanged between Ajay, Binki, and Sunil. Then, she entered Randhira in her posh nightgown. No words were spoken. They were only nodding their heads and acknowledging things with half-hearted smiles. Randhira approached Sunil amongst all this, but he turned away from her.

Everyone ate in silence. After eating, they waited until Satto Bibi and Porush entered. Everyone stood up when the two arrived.

"Please sit down; this is going to be a long conversation," the bald man dressed in black said.

The table was long and covered in white cloth. Sunil and Randhira sat on one side with a two-chair gap, and Ajay and Binki sat on the other side next to one another. Porush and Satto Bibi both sat at the head of the table so they could address them all.

"Last night was eventful," said Porush.

"Us getting stuck here is not a coincidence. Our car is missing, it is not a coincidence, so it's clear that you want something. What is it?" Sunil asked bluntly.

"Money. What else could it be?" Randhira spoke in arrogance and rolled her eyes.

Porush smiled and waited, "No, Ms Bajaj, it is not." He answered with a straight face.

Ajay and Binki looked at Porush.

Porush turned to Ajay and Binki. "I didn't know how else to answer that," he said to Ajay and Binki, shrugging his shoulders.

"Didn't confirm my surname this time, either?" Asked Randhira.

Porush again chose not to react to her childishness and remained assertive.

"We are going to finish what we started last night. Like or not, Ms Bajaj... you are marrying Mr Grewal."

"What makes you think I want to marry a woman that doesn't want to marry me?" Asked Sunil.

"We have no choice but to go ahead with you, Mr Grewal. Time is running out."

"Go with me? What do you mean by that?"

"You see…and I am sure you are aware of it too."

"Aware of what?" Asked Sunil.

"Ms Bajaj's track record."

Sunil looked at her, and Randhira was embarrassed, too.

Sunil took a deep sigh, "Yes."

"You are. We have been watching Ms Bajaj for a long time and know of all her relationships before she met you.

"How?" Randhira asked.

"Besides the point," Satto Bibi muttered.

"So? What does that have to do with anything?" Asked Randhira.

"Everything," answered Porush. "And out of all her relationships, we believed she is truly in love with you, Mr Grewal, and if she would end up marrying anyone, it would be you. But then we all saw what happened last night."

No one said anything.

"You are a decent man, Mr Grewal, and if anyone can still love Randhira despite all her shortcomings, it is you," said Satto Bibi.

"Shortcomings?! How dare you, you old woman!" Randhira got up and shouted.

"*Chup kar! Holi Bol!* Sit down!" Satto Bibi stood and shouted at Randhira.

"What have I done to you? Why do you all hate us?" Asked Randhira. Sunil was next to stand up.

"Everyone, please calm down and sit back down!" Porush brought the session to order without getting up.

"We don't hate you, Mr. Grewal...but..."

"...But you hate me!" Exclaimed Randhira.

"Let's put it this way...we don't exactly love you after..."

"After what?" Sunil interrupted Porush.

"In good time," Porush regathered himself.

"No! I am getting sick and tired! I want to know!" Sunil shouted this time.

"Taking turns, are you both?" Satto Bibi asked.

"Mr Grewal, silence! No shouting!" Porush raised his voice.

Sunil sat down, staring hard at Satto Bibi and Porush. By this time, Satto Bibi and Randhira had both sat down.

"Mr Grewal, have you heard the term, let sleeping dogs lie?"

"Yes."

"Right! Then let us leave sleeping dogs lie for now and concentrate on getting you both married."

"Why?"

"Do you still love her?" asked Ajay.

Sunil got emotional. "Yes."

Randhira's eyes began to water at Sunil's magnanimity and nobility.

"After last night, Sunil?" Randhira was shocked and in awe of her man.

"I still love you," Sunil turned to Randhira. "And I would marry you, despite last night."

"Excellent; in that case, the problem is solved. As I said, you are a great man, Mr Grewal. Now, please give me and Satto Bibi some time in private with Ms Bajaj," implored Porush.

"What is there that I cannot know?" Sunil asked.

"Please, Mr Grewal, I want you to find everything at the appropriate time and from the appropriate person. I'm afraid that is not me," said Porush. "But before you go, I would like to ask Ms Bajaj, after hearing that you would still marry her…would she still marry you?"

Randhira pondered and said, "Yes."

"She changed her mind fast!" Mocked Binki. She was unconvinced by Randhira.

"Mrs Pranjpe! Please…" Porush again implored.

Randhira remembered the name. Ajay Pranjpe was one of the elite businessmen in the capital city. He was not necessarily a friend of her father's, but he was well known. She may have met him once or twice, but not enough to remember him. As Porush said the surname, Randhira remembered who he was. But the question was... *what was he doing here*, she thought?

"That is enough for us. They are ready to get married, and then the problem can be resolved peacefully," Satto Bibi said.

"What problem?" Asked Sunil.

"All you need to worry about, Mr Grewal, is that you are getting married tonight," confirmed Porush.

"Now! If everyone would please... leave apart from Ms Bajaj," requested Porush.

Ajay and Binki stood up and left. Sunil, too, followed.

"Ajay, please make sure Mr Grewal doesn't eavesdrop," Porush instructed, and Ajay nodded and adhered.

Porush waited for them to leave and then asked his question.

"Right then, Renu *Bhabhi*! Shall we start?" Porush spoke as he slouched back in his seat, folded his arms, and smiled.

"*Bhabhi*? I am not related to you. I am not your sister-in-law!" Randhira said, grinding her teeth.

"Really? After seeing my brother's painting in the gallery, you say this?" Asked Porush.

"I never married your brother!"

"If you ended up marrying him, you'd become my *Bhabhi*. But, of course, we all know what you think of marriage!" mocked Porush.

Randhira sat there, crumbling her hands together.

"Fine! We had a passing affair. So what? Everyone does. We were young and at university," blurted Randhira.

"Did you love him?" Asked Satto Bibi.

Porush held his hand out to Satto Bibi.

Randhira thought, "I liked him, he was fun. He was handsome."

"He loved you! With all his heart!" Satto Bibi shouted.

"He was soft!" Randhira came back at her.

"He was from the village. Everyone from the village wears their hearts on their sleeves," Porush clarified.

"It's about time they stopped doing this, for everyone's sake!" Randhira shouted again.

Porush shook his head in frustration and disbelief and asked, "Do you have any remorse?"

"For what? For being in a relationship with someone that could not handle a breakup?"

"Why did you break up with him?"

"He wanted to get married after university; I was too young and unprepared!"

"You still aren't prepared, but you're not young anymore," Satto Bibi broke in.

If looks could cause harm, Satto Bibi would have been severely injured by Randhira's glare after having commented on her age.

"Listen, me getting married…how does that benefit you? Let us both go. I will make sure my father pays you millions of rupees," Randhira tried to strike a deal.

Porush and Satto Bibi looked at one another and did not display their anger at the offer.

"All right! Let's go back. What do you know? What do you think happened to Aaroush after you met him for the last time?"

"I didn't know until I saw his portrait, and you said he had departed," Randhira said numbly, as though she were concerned.

"And you never tried to find out?"

"I may have called once or twice?"

"Ah yes…two years after your meeting, when you had supposedly met for the last time, you decided to check up on him. You didn't love him, did you?"

"Listen, whether I did or not, I don't know…We met on the first day of university and became friends. We were eighteen or nineteen."

"He told us."

"I want to hear it from her, Porush," Satto Bibi said.

"University life is so fast. Everything is like a long intoxication. It's like ecstasy. Whom we meet, what we do, and what we say all get forgotten because it is one thing after another. Everything happens so fast. Some boys and girls had seen freedom for the first time. Girls had their hostels, and Boys had theirs. But we all arranged to meet after our classes."

"We are listening."

"Aaroush was a great person. I loved him as a friend. I could talk to him about everything. He'd protect me from bad company and keep me out of trouble. He'd help me with my homework and coursework. We studied together. We hung out together. He was an exceptional student. He was handsome. Everything about him was amazing. Although I knew he was from the village, our thoughts, and lifestyles would never match, and I couldn't help but be attracted to him. He, too, liked me, and we became an item."

"Go on."

"For most of the first year, we were together, and then, everyone broke up for the end of year break."

"But you asked him to meet you just a week later and called him to the capital city."

"Yes."

"Why?"

"Didn't he tell you?"

"We want to hear it from you."

"Fine! I met him to tell him I was three months pregnant."

"You were pregnant at university and didn't tell him."

"I wasn't sure. I thought it was just a hiccup in my cycles."

"So, you met up."

"I told him the children are his and that I'd have to give birth; otherwise, the complications could be severe, and I could lose my life. I told him that my mother is planning to take me away as soon as it's safe for me to travel abroad where I can give birth and that I have to give the children to him once they're born and…"

"…And the key thing you didn't say."

"…I was about to," Randhira again ground her teeth.

"Go on then."

Randhira huffed and said, "He said let's get married, but I told him that I could not marry him."

"So, you went away abroad, gave birth, brought the children back, and got in touch with him again, and he met you in a hotel room in the capital city? Right?" Asked Porush.

"How do you know about the hotel room?"

"Because my parents came with him. They were in his room. You invited him to yours."

"I don't know of that."

"Did you notice any changes in him?"

"Of course! He was disheartened, deflated, and punctured. He had started to lose his hair and had this awful thick beard. He looked terrible. He looked unwell."

"Yes, because his will to live was gone when you said you won't marry him. That killed him!"

Randhira began to cry.

"I didn't want this for him."

"What did you do when you met him."

"I handed the children to him and bid farewell. I was going back abroad to finish my education."

"He asked you again in the hotel room to marry him?"

"Yes, and I said no," Randhira cried.

"Out of the two, the boy is eldest, isn't he?" Satto Bibi asked.

"By two minutes, yes."

"Didn't I say your firstborn would be a boy?" Satto Bibi said.

Randhira looked at Satto Bibi with fixed eyes.

"So…you left him with two babies?"

"Yes."

"Do you know what happened after that?"

"No."

"He took them to his room, where our parents were, and he collapsed. He could not bear your loss. He could not bear to see you leave him forever," Porush continued.

"I can imagine what he must have gone through. I saw his painting and now know he is no more. I am hurt," Randhira said.

"Hurt! Rubbish! You are the one responsible for his death!" Satto Bibi shouted.

"I didn't mean any of this to happen, I assure you," Randhira cried more.

Porush and Satto Bibi, too, started to weep.

"You know what it did to our family? It broke us!" Porush cried.

"I am so sorry, I didn't know he would end up dying in grief," Randhira said.

"But you didn't even try to find out."

"I called after two years, but the phone just rang and rang," cleared Randhira.

"He was long dead by then," Satto Bibi said while crying.

Randhira wept more. "I am so sorry."

Porush cleared his throat and said, "During the first year of university, during the early breaks, he'd come home. He'd show us your photos and talk to everyone about you day and night. He'd talk to our parents, Satto Bibi, and Bansi Baba."

"You killed my grandson, Renu!" Satto Bibi blamed Randhira.

"We would sit down after evening meals, and he'd talk about you nonstop. Telling us how wonderful you are. How beautiful you are," Porush went on. "Call us stupid, Ms Bajaj, but when we love someone, us villagers, we love them with all our hearts and can do anything for that person."

"That's not the case with you!" Satto Bibi exclaimed. "When he collapsed in the hotel, my son, and daughter had to carry him back. He would not eat, sleep, or drink, and eventually, he died!" Satto Bibi wept.

"My mother couldn't withstand the shock and died two days after his funeral. My father went a year after my mother. Our family was ruined," Porush, too, was crying. "But Satto Bibi, Bansi Baba, and I had to be strong for the two babies."

"Where are they?" Randhira asked timidly.

"We thought you never ask, you hard-hearted woman!" Shouted Satto Bibi.

"Please! Please! Don't say that," Randhira said.

"You're first born...we named him after you, Randhir. He..."

"He...? Tell me what happened to him."

"He must be kept confined. From birth, he was declared mental."

Randhira cried even more upon hearing that.

"With good care, he can get better, but he needs specialist care," Satto Bibi explained.

"It might be a bit too late for that now, Bibi. It's been left too late," Porush followed up.

"And my daughter?"

"You have met her,"

"The girl that looks like me?" Ameeran? She? She is my daughter?" Randhira had happiness on her face.

"Yes."

They all cried for a little longer together and then went silent.

"Why do you want me to marry Sunil?" Randhira asked, breaking the silence, and wiping her tears. Her internal conflict erupted, desiring the answer.

Porush, too, composed himself and stopped crying. "Satto Bibi and Bansi Baba are dying. They don't have long to live. As for me, I am not married, so we want you to take care of your children from now on."

"Why marriage? Why Sunil?"

"There are two reasons. Firstly, Satto Bibi and Bansi Baba do not have time for you to break up with Mr Grewal, find someone else, and fall in love with that person. If there is anyone who would still love you enough after knowing this, it is Mr Grewal. He will understand and support you on this."

"Second?"

"He."

"Who?"

"He will not let you leave here in one piece."

"Who?"

"Whom did you encounter last night?

"The lion?"

"Yes, the lion. You see, I don't know if Aaroush told you or not, but he and the lion grew up together. He has been his companion until my brother went to university," Porush explained.

"Oh yes, he said he has a best friend back home that he'd like me to meet someday. I used to get jealous. I thought I was his best friend. At times, I thought there was another girl in his life! He meant the lion?"

"Yes, when Aaroush was a child, he found a lion cub in the jungle whose parents had died along with their other cubs. The entire pride had died due to unknown circumstances. The cub was the lone survivor. Aaroush brought it home; we looked after it all together. Aaroush even gave it his name. We'd feed it, give it milk, and he became family. He grew and became our protector. He wouldn't let any harm to any of us; however, the unfortunate part was…"

"…What was that?" Asked Randhira.

"He knows about you. Aaroush, during his holidays, would tell everyone about you, including him. He showed him your photos. Aaroush had a put up a photo of you in his room." Satto Bibi said.

"The day we brought Aaroush's ashes home, the lion went inside our home, which he never does, took your photograph from Aaroush's room, brought it outside, dropped it on the ground, placed his sharp, strong paw on it, and tore it up. After witnessing that, we understood that if anyone hated you enough to cause you harm, it was him. Because no matter how much we hate you... *Bhabhi*... we won't harm you. After all, you are the mother of my brother's children and hopefully will take care of them after Satto Bibi and Bansi Baba. I would have taken care of them, but we are from a village near the capital; my brother must have mentioned it to you. I am single. I can barely support myself. Ateet is just a setup that we used to lure you in."

"I would like to know how you lured us in," Randhira said assertively.

"Ajay and Binki will tell you," Said Porush.

"Of course... them!"

"But right now, if you want Aaroush to spare you, then drop this arrogance. Take responsibility for your children, give them a good life, marry Sunil, and by seeing this, he will, I'm sure, let you live," Porush said.

"I am to tell Sunil this…My God!"

"That we leave up to you. How you wish to lay the foundations of your marriage is up to you. In any case, you must tell him about the children because you will take them with you."

"Why marriage?"

"Marriage commitment will prove you are ready to take responsibility, and maybe by seeing you have done that, he may spare you for the children."

"He is an animal! What does he know? He won't be at the wedding!"

"Did he not stop when I told him to?"

"If he hates me, why didn't he tear me to shreds last night?"

"Maybe he wants to give you a chance?"

"He is an animal, Porush! Animals cannot think like that!"

"How can you be so sure? He could have killed any of us a long time ago. Animals have feelings. They understand."

"Why did he go for Sunil?"

"I don't know... maybe he didn't like someone else standing in Aaroush's stead."

"What guarantee is there that he will spare us?"

"There isn't. I, Satto Bibi and Bansi Baba, will explain and implore him to let you go."

"Porush, this sounds so ridiculous!" Randhira shouted.

"*Bhabhi*, he listened to me last night! What more proof do you want? He listens to us."

"What if he still doesn't?"

Porush shrugged his shoulders.

"What does that mean?

"If you leave with the children and get married, he might forgive you and let you go, but..."

"But what?"

"If you leave here without the children and getting married, he will come after you. The choice is yours."

Chapter 6: Ajay and Binki

Randhira nodded her head, wiped her tears dry, got up from her seat, and left the dining room to find Ajay, Binki, and Sunil standing in the lobby. She went straight up to Ajay and Binki and asked, "Can we please talk?"

"Would anyone tell me what the fuck is going on here? Why are you crying, Renu? What did they say?" Sunil asked.

Randhira turned to Sunil, held both his hands, and replied, "Sunil, please give me a little bit more time. I will tell you everything. Sit here and wait for me. Trust me."

Sunil slumped his shoulders again, ran his fingers through his hair, and nodded.

Randhira turned to Ajay and Binki and asked, "Shall we?"

Ajay and Binki exchanged looks before nodding, and the three went into a nearby meeting room, leaving Sunil distraught. Sunil sat down on one of the lobby armchairs and glared in disbelief at the ground. Bansi walked by and observed this, shook his head at the situation, and walked into the dining room, where Satto Bibi and Porush were still sitting. Bansi made eye contact with Satto and Porush and lifted his head. The gesture asked the question, "How did it go?"

"It went well, everything is cleared, and she knows everything," Porush said.

"I think everything will be all right; I mean, after knowing…"

"…After knowing she has children, instead of running to them and embracing them, she has gone to speak with Ajay and Binki, hah!" Bansi finished Satto's sentence in his old, harsh, and croaky voice.

He walked slowly towards the kitchen with his hands behind his back and coughed hard.

"Baba, are you all right?" Porush Asked.

Bansi coughed more, shook his head, and continued to slouch, walking off towards the kitchen with his hands behind his back.

"Where is your walking stick?" Satto Bibi asked her husband.

"It is good to walk without it sometimes," Bansi responded.

"I am positive she will realize her mistake and accept responsibility," Porush said.

Bansi stopped and turned toward his wife and grandson, giving a shunning expression, and waving his hand at them in a rejecting gesture.

"What does that mean?" Asked Porush.

"He is saying she will not take any responsibility," Satto Bibi told Porush.

"Calamity will fall! Be prepared," Bansi warned and turned to walk off; a smirk graced his lips.

"Stop being so negative, Baba!" Porush shouted. "After all these years, something good is about to happen."

"*Oye*, you stupid boy!" Bansi raised his voice. "I have more years on you. I know how this will end."

"Tell me then, Baba, how?" Porush folded his arms.

"Satto, tell him, please," Bansi turned to his wife.

"Why are you saying this?" Satto Bibi asked her husband.

"You don't believe me? Fine, get their car and leave it outside, and go tell her their car is ready for them before she gets married," Basni replied.

"I can do that; what difference will that make?" Porush questioned.

"You don't think she'll try to run?" Bansi asked rhetorically.

"Never, she will not leave her children behind," Porush answered with confidence,

"*Oye beta, oye* my naïve innocent boy! You have fallen for her crocodile tears. You have so much confidence in that woman! She is a cobra! She is whom we all despised two days ago. If you have so much confidence in her, give them their car. Don't tell Sunil. Tell her. Bring their car out to the front. Then watch what she does."

"You think she will run?" Porush asked again.

"Why? Lost your so-called belief in her? Lost the confidence in her? Hah!" Bansi mocked.

Porush remained silent.

"Yes! Yes! You have no answer for me because deep down, you know she is capable," Bansi finished.

"But…"

"…*Oye…beta ji*…Do whatever the hell you both want to!" Bansi interrupted with a raised voice and began to jeer under his breath as he walked away. Satto Bibi and Porush stood there in silence.

"Don't give the keys, Porush," Satto Bibi commanded.

"No, I will."

"Your Baba may be right; she can run," said Satto Bibi.

"We must trust her if she is to care for the children. We need to make sure she won't put them up for adoption once she reaches the capital city."

"She can do that when she gets there, no?" Asked Satto Bibi.

"If she doesn't run and gets married, then it will give us some hope that she will take care of her children and keep her marriage," Porush said.

"But then it might not get to that if she runs," Satto Bibi said.

"He won't let her go," Porush answered sternly.

"We cannot rely on Aaroush to stop her. She might get away, and then what?"

"Impossible! Did Aaroush not stop them yesterday? Aaroush will not let them leave! Not without the children, at least."

"Have you reasoned with Aaroush yet?"

Porush pondered before answering, "No, not yet, because I wanted to reason with him after the marriage. But Baba has now put all these concerns in my head!"

"What you Baba say is often right, as much as I hate to admit. But no, you mustn't give them the keys. Let this marriage take place," Satto implored.

"No…I will give them their car."

"Why make this option available?" Asked Satto Bibi.

"Now I understood what Baba was trying to say," Porush spoke with understanding.

"What?"

"To truly test someone's intentions, we must present them with two paths, right and wrong. Then, we must leave it up to them to choose which they tread," Porush said and stormed out of the dining room.

***

In the other meeting room, Ajay and Binki faced a hot-headed Randhira.

"So, tell me then, you both," Randhira folded her arms and spoke.

"First of all, please mind your tone," Ajay cleared.

Randhira looked away in anger and took a deep breath.

"You know what I want to know," Randhira told them.

"And we don't have to tell you anything," Binki said.

"Mrs. Binki Pranjpe, sorry, Mrs Manisha Pranjpe. I should have known from the start. I have seen you at many parties, but my father didn't find you both important enough. That's why he never considered introducing you to me," Randhira jeered.

"He has introduced us to you, and if we know you well, then you will remember too," Binki said.

Ajay took a deep breath and said, swallowing the insult, "For me, this conversation is over." Ajay began to walk off.

"No wait…I am sorry. Please, I need to know," Randhira begged.

"…How you ended up here? Because of us, you stupid bitch, and guess what… we will not tell you how. Do you know why? Because we are insignificant!" Yelled Binki.

"I am sorry. Please!" Randhira again begged.

"I am not entertaining anymore of your tantrums, Ms Bajaj," Ajay warned.

Randhira nodded and said, "Please, I need to know how…"

"No, I shouldn't have said that. I am sorry," Randhira apologized; her stomach felt as if it dropped to the floor.

"Away with you, Randhira Bajaj! Go to all the significant businesspeople. They will help you find out how we helped these poor people," Binki said, still angry.

"I implore you! I am sorry, please tell me," Randhira asked.

"I think she has a right to know, Binki," Ajay said to his wife.

"Oh please, Ajju! You are so soft! She called you insignificant!"

"I know I am not insignificant, and you do too, so why mind what this stupid girl has to say about us," Ajay cleared. "She needs to grow up."

Randhira wanted to call him a bastard for calling her a stupid girl but kept mum because she needed to know.

"Please tell me," Randhira begged.

"Ajay, I don't want to be in her presence any longer than I need to be. So, keep it short," Binki told Ajay.

"Fine," Ajay said and gestured towards the sofas in the meeting room.

All three sat down to talk.

"Porush got in touch and told me what had happened to Aaroush and what happened between you both. He told me about the children and asked if we could help track you down. This was two years after you both had supposedly broken up. It was after you left those missed calls on Aaroush's phone."

"Porush could have called me himself," Randhira asked,

"I don't know why he didn't. Maybe he was too afraid to hear what you would say. In honesty, I don't know."

"Then?"

"I knew who you were, and I had a private detective follow you for three months. At that time, you were with Manoj. I think after Aaroush, you started seeing Manoj."

"Yes, I met him when I was abroad. We happened to be from the same capital city back home."

"You broke up with him," Ajay stated.

"Yes."

"Why?"

"Didn't the detective tell you?" She stiffened her spine.

"Oh, come on, Ajju. He must have asked her to marry him, and she said no," Binki jumped in.

Randhira clenched her fist but soon released it because she knew Binki was right.

"We are going on a tangent. I told Porush and gave him photos of the investigation, and he asked me to stop it. He said you had moved on. Porush, Satto Bibi, and Bansi Baba were happy to bring up the children, but they didn't know of Randhir's condition at the time," Ajay said.

"Even when they did find out, they didn't try to find Randhira," Binki added.

"Yes, I know. Only when both Bansi Baba and Satto Bibi fell ill did Porush reach out to me again."

"How do you and they know of my track record?"

"I told them of your track record. How did I find out? Your family is well known in the capital city's top elite business circle, and you are their daughter. I don't think there was an event you missed. We went to most business events held in the capital city. Whenever I saw you with someone new, I made a mental note. Then, I made light inquiries about the person you were seeing. I didn't go out of my way. I tried hard not to be too invasive. Just his name and who he was."

"Or she," Binki added again. Ajay elbowed Binki gently.

"What do you mean by that?" Randhira pretended she did not know what Binki meant.

"Please, I know about you and Smita Handa." Ajay again gently nudged Binki when she said this.

"That was just a phase!" Randhira spoke under her breath.

"It's none of our business, Binki. I kept Smita Handa off your track record list. Porush and his family do not know," Ajay explained. "Whether Sunil knows or not, I don't know, I don't care. He won't know through us. We are not going to mention it."

Randhira nodded in gratitude.

"But just to finish off what I was saying. I watched for what you were doing and whom you were seeing. That's all," Ajay finished.

"That's horrible. Why would you do that?" Randhira asked.

"Yes, I know I am not proud of that. But in case Porush wanted to know, I ensured I had that information."

"But why? Why help them? It couldn't have been for money."

"No, not everything is about money, Randhira," Ajay smiled.

"Why then?"

"I was in the boy's hostel like Aaroush at university. I can't say we were friends because you would have known me. But yes, we knew each other. We used to say hello whenever we passed each other in the corridor."

"So, you knew him…that was it?"

"That was not all, of course not. It was during the first early reading week in the first year that my parents and siblings were away for that week. They had booked a vacation, and it was booked long in advance. They thought I would be away at university, so they booked the trip. I couldn't go home because no one would have been there. Aaroush saw me sitting alone in my room when everyone was headed home for the week, and he came into my room and asked when I was leaving. I told him I was not and would spend reading week mostly alone at university. He asked me to come along to his house. I went with him, and the love his parents and his grandparents gave me was incredible. I was so overwhelmed."

"You never got close?"

"For some strange reason, no. After having stayed with his family for an entire week. I don't know why. Maybe I should have tried. After that one week, we all went back to our friend's circle and our groups. But we'd always stop to catch up when we'd bump into each other in the corridors and talk. I'd ask about his family. I'd ask him about Aaroush, the lion."

"You are known to the lion?"

"When Porush got in touch, I went to their home outside the capital city. The lion recognized me.

Which made things easier when this location was chosen."

"So, you owed Aaroush one?"

"You can say that, and when Porush contacted me the second time to locate you, I couldn't say no?"

"So, tell me how you did this."

"Ateet is one of my projects. We are making a resort here. Did your father ever mention the Jopa Resort Project?"

"It will become the biggest project ever in North India! My father is a shareholder, and he said the owner will become the richest man in North India after this project."

Ajay's lips upturned.

"You are the owner? Oh my!"

"No, we are insignificant, aren't we, Ajju?" Binki laughed.

"I am so sorry, Binki, sorry…ma'am, if I had known…"

"…Ma'am… *Uff*," Binki placed her arm on her head and dramatically fell backwards onto the sofa.

"Ajju, gather me; I am about to faint. Randhira Bajaj just called me ma'am, ha-ha," chuckled Binki while performing her theatrics.

"Binki, come on, please." Ajay's brows furrowed, giving a warning not to try to perform her dramatic gesture.

"Sorry, I couldn't help it. Yes, Randhira Bajaj, your father has invested in this project," Ajay explained.

"But he didn't tell me about it? I know of it, but never saw any photos of the location or went into any details..."

"...That's not the point here. I guess you not knowing much about it helped us. The business deal happened recently and extremely quickly, so we are overwhelmed by everything that is going on, but as soon as Porush called me, I put everything on hold and focused on this."

Randhira lowered her eyes.

"It was simple, Randhira. We hired the same detective. He has been watching you for the last three months. We knew you were going to Sunil's sister's *Rokka*. Coincidentally, Sandali, who is Sunil's sister, her fiancé... is known to me," Ajay said.

"Excellent, and he didn't invite you to the *Rokka*?" Randhira asked.

"Randhira, in case you don't know, *Rokka* is a ceremony for the immediate family only."

"But the rich have a big celebration for their *Rokka*."

"Why are you asking me? Ask Sunil," Ajay laughed.

"Did you tell Sandali's fiancé everything?"

"No! I wouldn't do that. However, I told him to stay there longer, spend time with Sandali's family, and get to know them better, which…"

"…delayed us!"

"Precisely. I didn't tell him anything about anything, so don't worry. But our aim was that you left late. We knew the date. And after what I told him to do, we knew you'd be driving down through this area late at night," Ajay Continued.

"And why this location?" Randhira inquired.

"Ateet used to be a guesthouse; the purchase was complete. We modified it slightly for your stay and set it up on all the booking websites."

"How did you know we'd book this?"

"Was there any other hotel or guesthouse nearby?"

"Nothing showed up apart from Ateet?"

"Exactly. With the help of some influential people in this area and top hotel booking websites in this country, I convinced all the hotels, guesthouses, beds, and breakfasts to go offline for that evening. We asked even the smallest of places where someone could stay for the night to go offline or be unavailable. Only this part was tough. My team had to make some phone calls, call in some favors, and make some payments. In any case, we got what we wanted - the only place you could book for that night was Ateet."

"What of the reviews? How did you set them up? There were both good ones and bad ones?" Randhira Asked.

And one said, "Once you stayed here, you cannot go back. Or something like that."

"This is funny," Ajay smiled, and Binki started laughing.

"When we purchased it and visited for the first time, we saw, at the entrance of Ateet, a board which read, *"Mehman aata apni marzi se hai par jata mehezbaan ki marzi se hai!"*

Binki laughed more.

"This was at the guesthouse's entrance. When Binki and I read it, we laughed. We were on the floor. I can understand what the previous owner was trying to do. I can understand he was trying to be sweet because if you say it in Hindi, it sounds so welcoming and warm. But it sounds so creepy in English. We just removed that and just wrote, *"Ateeti Devo Bhava!"*

"But we found it so funny, and…and…we used that phrase to scare you and Sunil when you guys arrived, and so did Satto Bibi," laughed Binki, and Ajay laughed with her. "You can only leave when we will allow you to."

"I'm not laughing!" Randhira interjected.

"Sorry."

"But the reviews…"

"What about them? All places have good and bad reviews. We tried to set it up so it looked genuine."

"It said something in those lines in English in the reviews. That could have deterred me."

"Really?" Ajay was shocked. I will check. We asked Zippy to put some bad reviews in there. But it was silly for him to put that down. Must have been a mistake on his side."

"He can be so stupid sometimes! Stupid boy!" Binki commented. "I'm going to slap him! Next time I meet him."

"No need. Binki, Sunil, and Randhira booked Ateet, and the task was done. It was the only one in the area. They weren't deterred," Ajay explained.

"We were lucky, though," Binki said.

"Who is Zippy?" Randhira asked.

"Hacker, sorry, IT whiz kid. We hired one from the capital city."

"How?"

"Easy peasy; lemon squeezy! You can find one at every corner," Binki winked at Randhira.

"And our car?" Randhira asked.

"How hard is it to start a car without its keys, Randhira?" Binki said.

"It was moved carefully to a nearby safe yet discreet location. No damage to it was done," Ajay assured.

"Who moved it?" Randhira questioned.

"Does that matter?" Ajay answered.

"Our phones, tablets, landlines?" Randhira continued to ask.

Ajay raised his eyebrows.

"Oh yes, how difficult is it to jam the network these days?"

"Precisely!"

"Money, Randhira! Spend it wisely, and it can work in your favor," Binki smiled again.

"Or use it to repay others' favor…in your case!" Randhira uttered.

"Call it what you may, Ms Bajaj," Binki shrugged.

"My father will be so angry!" Randhira threatened.

"It's best not to tell him because if you do, we will return his money, and he will no longer be a shareholder."

Randhira's face dropped. "But you need his money, right, for the project?"

"Hah! No, Mr Jai Kishen Ram Ganesh Shankar is ready to invest double the amount," Ajay disclosed.

"I love his name," Binki said.

"Let me clear it up. His name is Jai Kishen. Ram is his father's name; Ganesh is his grandfather's name and…"

"…yes, Shankar is his surname," Binki interposed. "He is such a nice chap! Shall we just go with him and return Mr Bajaj's money?"

"We can do that," Ajay responded to Binki.

"And if he asks why, then we can say we met his daughter and tell him how rude…sorry, nice she was to us," Binki told Ajay.

"Please…no one needs to know," Randhira mentioned.

"We thought so. Let's not involve anyone else. Enough people are involved already," Ajay said and stood up. Binki and Randhira, too, followed suit.

"Wait, I want to know why you asked us to leave as soon as possible on the first day?" Randhira asked Binki. "And why did you act weirdly in the lifts the following morning? And you, Ajay told Sunil he should have driven off the following day when we returned. Why?"

"The aim was to make you feel uncomfortable. I don't exactly remember what I said," said Ajay,

"Me neither," Binki followed up. "The main aim was to scare you a little."

"And what if we left straight away?"

"Your car was removed as soon as you entered Ateet."

"Porush reacted badly to what I was asking you in the lift," Randhira said to Binki.

"All a part of the act," said Ajay.

"So why did they say we must ask for Satto Bibi's permission and that we weren't allowed to stay outside wedlock?"

"Now that was done so that Sunil gets to know your real thoughts about marriage," Binki explained.

"You could have ruined our relationship!" Randhira spoke.

Ajay did not say anything, and neither did Binki.

"One more thing? How did you transport the lion here to this location?"

"Mr Anand Gupta from the capital city zoo he is…"

"…known to you, of course," Randhira finished Ajay's sentence and rolled her eyes.

"He made the arrangements. Aaroush didn't just turn up and happened to be there last night. It was all set up. Lion tamers and professional zookeepers have set their base in the woods and closely monitor all activities outside Ateet. They have been looking after Aaroush. When they saw you were leaving, they released him," Ajay said.

Randhira was astonished at the planning depth.

"Not so insignificant after all, eh?" Binki showed off, bringing her shoulders back.

Then, there was a knock at the door, and Porush was there.

"May I come, I promise I didn't hear anything."

"Come in, Porush," Binki said.

"Oh, so you must have told her about…"

"…Yes, she knows."

Porush nodded and gave a faint smile.

"Tonight, you're getting married, yes?" Porush asked.

"I haven't spoken to Sunil yet."

"Oh."

"If we've gauged him well enough, he will still marry you." An awkward silence followed after Porush said this.

"You didn't ask to meet the children? Randhir? Or you didn't ask for Ameeran? Shall I call them?" Porush said.

Randhira tried hard to put on a false smile.

"Of course… I'd… I'd love to… meet them, but I think I should speak with Sunil first."

Porush nodded.

"Mother's heart has not called out yet, no?" Binki asked with a cunning smile.

"Ma'am, Porush, it is not like that?" Randhira said, trying hard to smile.

Porush turned to Binki and asked, "Ma'am?"

"Long and funny story!" Binki laughed.

Porush smiled and closed his eyes.

"Anyway, I know, I'm sure you'll love them and take good care of your children," Porush said.

Randhira again tried hard to smile.

"*Ek maa ka dil.* Oh, a mother's heart! Ouch!" Binki laughed out loud, mocking her.

Randhira's smile faded away. Ajay smirked at Binki's comment. Porush could not contain his grin either.

"Binki *Bhabhi*, please," Porush said.

"Sorry," Binki said, trying to contain her laughter.

"Anyways, Renu *Bhabhi*, in your own time," Porush turned to Randhira. "Speak to Mr Grewal. I only came to say one thing."

"What was that?" Randhira asked.

"We found your car. It is parked at the front and ready for you this evening."

Randhira turned actively towards Porush like a drowning man was thrown a lifeline—a drowning woman in this case.

"Really?" she asked. "You found it?"

"You know what I mean, Renu *Bhabhi*," Porush answered.

Ajay and Binki's faces turned extremely serious, and they stared hard at Porush with widened eyes and disbelief.

"Yes, it is ready for you. So, when you marry tonight, you can leave with your children."

Randhira nodded in alertness.

"I will speak with Sunil now, so please excuse me," Randhira said, swiftly exiting the room.

"Are you crazy, Porush?" Ajay walked over to Porush hastily after Randhira left. Ajay grabbed his arm tightly and turned him towards himself.

"That was too soon. You should wait for the marriage," Binki advised.

"No, I think the time is right. I want to see what she does," Porush answered, intrigued about her next move.

"They will run, that's what she will do!" Binki shouted.

"He won't let them,"

"We cannot rely on the lion," Ajay said.

"Aaroush," Porush corrected him, which wasn't his typical demeanor.

"You know I didn't mean it like that, Porush, but she may convince Sunil to run," Ajay said.

"Even if she convinces Sunil, the poor chap will meet his end at the jaws of that beast."

Porush gently removed Ajay's hand kindly from his arm and held his hand in his own.

"Ajay *Bhaiya*, we make our own decision, and if Sunil decides to run away with her, he must take responsibility for his actions and be prepared to face the consequences."

Ajay shook his head vigorously.

"Let's be positive, Ajay *Bhaiya*, Binki *Bhabhi*. Let's hope they get dressed and come down to the altar, choose the right path, instead of choosing the wrong path by running away and leaving the children behind."

"And if they don't come down to the altar, and try to run? Do we stop them?"

"Na… She knows if they run, death stands at that gate out there."

Chapter 7: Randhira

Randhira wiped her tears and marched into the lobby from the meeting room. Although angry at the revelations made by everyone, she was ecstatic after finding out their car was outside. Sniffling still from the crying, she looked around the lobby. She searched for Sunil. Thinking he may have gone upstairs, she hurried hastily across the lobby and headed towards lifts. Still, she stopped hard after hearing the horrid noise. She heard Satto Bibi's anklets.

"Where to in such a rush?" Satto Bibi asked.

Randhira had her back to Satto Bibi and rolled her eyes. She felt interrupted. She wiped her tears and turned to face Satto Bibi.

"I was going to…"

"…going meet Ameeran?" Satto Bibi asked softly with a smile.

Randhira waited for a while but answered without delay, "Yes! I was looking for her but want to meet her privately."

"I thought so. After all, you're a mother," Satto Bibi said, wrapping her arm around Randhira. Randhira was not used to this soft side of Satto Bibi.

"I haven't told Sunil yet, is he…?" Randhira asked.

Satto Bibi stopped and took her arm from Randhira's back. Satto Bibi was hurt at the fact she was asking for Sunil and not so eager to meet Ameeran after all. Satto Bibi stopped and looked at Randhira.

"Where is Sunil?" Randhira asked softly. "He was waiting here. I am just concerned. He hasn't gone out, has he? There is the lion outside," Randhira spoke quickly and timidly.

Satto Bibi smiled and nodded. "I told him to go upstairs to the Suite and that we'd send up his clothes."

Randhira nodded.

"Go upstairs to him. He should be there." Satto Bibi said.

"All right," Randhira said, wetting her lips with her tongue. She hated the taste of her tears.

Satto Bibi started to walk away.

"But you said you would take me to Randhir and Ameeran?" Questioned Randhira. Satto Bibi stopped and turned back towards her again and smiled with relief.

"Come with me; I will take you to Randhir first," said Satto Bibi, putting her arm around Randhira again. This time, Randhira smelled the burnt Sandalwood smell from Satto Bibi's hands, just as she had on the day they arrived.

"Let's go," Satto Bibi said to Randhira, walking off toward the gallery, and Randhira followed. There was a smell of dust in the gallery, which was neither pleasant nor unpleasant. Randhira ignored it, and Satto Bibi took her through the gallery, then the library, and then to a big, locked room. She pulled a chain around her neck from which a key hung. She took the chain off and slowly used the key to open the door quietly.

While Randhira waited, she looked around. She noticed a fire exit door beside it but could not tell where it led out. Satto Bibi opened the door to the room. She slid off her anklets from her feet and held them tight in her hands, avoiding the noise as she moved. Randhira found the room was stuffy and smelly. To her, it smelt like an occupied hospital ward. It had plenty of windows, so plenty of light shone through, but the room needed air. The smell was stifling. Randhira coughed gently after inhaling the air in the room. There was a bed in the middle of the room, and upon it lay asleep a teenager with long black hair and a long, thick beard. Randhira observed, and she saw his arm and leg were chained to the bed. She felt for the young man. But then Randhira looked out from the window. She saw the entrance of Ateet. She saw the dark purple BMW. She then could tell from standing within the room where the fire exit door led out. Her eyes lit up with delight, but she hid that from Satto Bibi.

Satto Bibi whispered to Randhira, "This is Randhir…your son."

Randhira looked at Satto Bibi and then at the boy in the bed expressionlessly.

"He suffers from a condition."

"What condition?"

"I don't know the name, but he is difficult to control. He is violent towards new people. That's why we've got him chained."

"Can we wake him up?" asked Randhira.

Satto Bibi looked around, sighed deeply, and said, "It's best not to."

Randhira nodded and looked back at the boy in the bed. She went up close; she could tell he had her features, even with his eyes closed. He shuffled slightly, and Randhira took a few steps back. Satto Bibi grabbed her wrist and quickly pulled her back.

"Let's go. Randhir should remain sedated," Satto Bibi said. She took Randhira out of the room, closed the doors quietly, gently turned the key to lock it, and hung the key around her neck once again.

"Does Ameeran suffer from any condition?" Randhira asked.

Satto Bibi gave a hesitant smile, hiding her disgust at the question.

"No, she can get enthusiastic and eccentric sometimes, but she is fine. She has taken after you."

Randhira nodded in relief.

"Let's go meet her," Satto said, headed back to where the lifts were and pressed the button to call it. The lift arrived, and the women got in. The ride up was silent. When the lift reached the top floor, they got out and headed to the room, where Randhira and Sunil saw Ameeran standing outside when they headed down on the first morning.

Ameeran looked at Randhira as she and Satto Bibi walked up to her. Satto Bibi gestured for Ameeran to go inside the room. Ameeran went inside, and Satto Bibi and Randhira followed them.

"Ameeran, this is your mother," Satto Bibi wasted no time.

Ameeran's eyes lit up with pleasure and shock, and a tear began to roll down her cheek. Upon seeing the happiness in the girl's eyes, Randhira's eyes also went wet. Ameeran swung her arms around Randhira, hugged her tightly, and cried. Randhira was at first hesitant but then gave in to the love and held the weeping girl.

"Oh, where have you been? Bibi and Porush Chacha said, one day you will come to get us, and look… you are here! Are you here to get us?" asked the excited Ameeran.

Randhira stepped back from the embrace but smiled and touched Ameeran's cheek.

"Yes, I have come to get you, *bachcha*," she replied.

Upon hearing this, Ameeran hugged Randhira again tightly. Satto Bibi, too, smiled in relief.

"Are we going now? Shall I pack? I haven't got anything ready!" Ameeran started to fluster in excitement.

"Relax, *bachcha*. We go tomorrow. Today, Satto Bibi and your Porush Chacha have arranged a ceremony for me and Uncle Sunil."

"Let's go now!" Ameeran said and turned to Satto Bibi. "Bibi, can we go now? Please? I am so happy I have finally got you." Ameeran turned back towards Randhira, held her again, and would not let go. She was like a child who had found her long-lost toy.

"Where were you for a long time? Why didn't you come and see us? Were you upset with us? I am sorry if I did anything wrong, but please don't leave us again," Ameeran said, getting emotional.

Randhira again held her gently and placed her hand on the girl's head.

"Shsh! All this can wait. I will tell you everything. We will leave tomorrow. We all need to get ready for the ceremony, and you need to pack, which will take time."

"And I still need to give your clothes to you..." Ameeran said and looked at Satto Bibi.

"...Don't worry, I'll do that; you can pack and prepare for the ceremony," Satto Bibi told Ameeran.

Ecstatic, Ameeran gave a little jump upon hearing that.

"We will go tomorrow, won't we?" Ameeran asked Randhira.

"Don't worry, don't cry. We'll all leave for the capital city together tomorrow morning," Randhira consoled the young girl. Satto Bibi nodded, and a faint smile appeared on her face. The innocent girl smiled back at Randhira's words. Randhira patted her back and leered at the young girl hesitantly.

"I will now get ready and speak to Uncle Sunil and…" She turned towards Satto Bibi.

"…I will bring your clothes. Give me an hour or so," Satto Bibi said.

"Yes, we all need to look good at the ceremony," Randhira smiled again unconvincingly at Satto Bibi.

Satto Bibi nodded again. Randhira left the room and headed to the Suite and down the corridor.

As Randhira left, Ameeran swung her arms around her great-grandmother and turned her around in happiness.

"Oh, I am so excited, Bibi!" Ameeran exclaimed.

Satto Bibi smiled and tapped her on her arms around her neck.

"Calm down, Ameeran, don't get too excited," Satto Bibi said.

"Oh, Bibi, you think she won't keep her promise, don't you?"

Satto Bibi shrugged her shoulders at the girl, and Ameeran let go of her.

"She said she would take us to the city tomorrow!"
The innocent girl said insistingly.

Satto Bibi gently touched her face, took a deep
breath, and held back her tears.

"Yes, my little kid, she will take you," Satto Bibi
said.

"Yes! Yes! Yes! Ameeran punched the air three
times and said, "I am going to start packing! Will
you pack Randhir's clothes, Bibi?"

Satto Bibi nodded and watched the young girl
bounce around the room. She danced and skipped
as she packed. Satto Bibi's eyes were now watery
with concern, and she wiped the only tear she could
not hold back and looked at the ceiling and said,

"God…Please help us. May all go well."

Satto Bibi put on her anklets, which she had held in
her hands the entire time. She left the room, too,
and saw Randhira walking ahead of her. Randhira
looked back as she heard the old woman's anklets.
Eventually, Randhira stopped outside the Suite,
waited for Satto Bibi to walk past, and got up to the
lift. Satto Bibi and pressed the button.

Randhira did not knock or go in until Satto Bibi had boarded the lift. As the lift arrived, Satto Bibi stared outwards into Randhira's eyes. She, too, was looking back directly at Satto Bibi without expression until the lift doors and cut eye contact for both.

Randhira took a deep breath as she stood outside the door to the Suite. She knew Sunil was inside. She ran her fingers through her hair, wiped any remaining tears from her eyes, and knocked on the door.

"Yes?" Randhira heard Sunil's voice from inside.

"It's me," Randhira spoke nervously yet loud enough so he could hear her.

The door opened, and she found standing a confounded Sunil. His eyes were slightly wet, and all Randhira could see was love in them for her. Randhira flung her arms around him and hugged him tight. He, too, hugged her tight, and both shared a gentle and loving kiss.

After the kiss, Randhira composed herself and walked in.

"Are you alright?" Sunil asked gently. His voice was calm, but emotions were trudging through a storm.

"I am fine, I guess. Are you?"

"Not really! No one is telling me what is going on."

"That's why I am here."

"Then please tell me."

Randhira sat down on the edge of the bed. "Come here," Randhira said, putting her hand on the bed and asking Sunil to come to sit beside her.

Sunil wasted no time, sat beside her, and turned slightly towards her. She grabbed his face in her soft hands.

"Now, Sunil, you have to believe what I am about to say and ask you to do," Randhira began.

"Go on," Sunil said.

"Do you promise, without any questions or hesitation, you will listen to me and, without any objection, do what I am proposing?

"It depends on what it is," Sunil answered.

"No, Sunil, I am serious about this. You must trust me on this one. Once we get back, I will answer all your questions, that I promise you," Randhira promised.

Sunil stared at Randhira expressionless. His face was still in her hands, and she brought his face nearer to hers and began to speak under her breath.

"We are trapped here…"

"…What?"

"Sh! Speak quietly," Randhira whispered. "Just listen to me very carefully."

"Okay," Sunil whispered back.

Randhira took her hands away from his face.

"We need to gather our things and quietly leave this room, go out to the end of this corridor, and quietly go down the stairs, making no noise. Once we reach the stairs below, we sneak into the gallery and the library. Before we get to the big room, a fire exit opens to the side of the front, which isn't far from the main entrance."

"Why are we sneaking out?" asked Sunil.

"Not yet. I will tell you in the car once we've set off. Right now, we need to get out of here."

"When are we going?"

"We'll do it when it's slightly dark. They are getting the altar ready for us."

"Again?"

"Yes. I want to marry you, but not like this. Let's get the fuck out of here. I will tell you everything. Just go with me on this. I will answer every question of yours."

"What do we do when we get to the front? Wait for the lion to come and eat us?"

"Shut up! We quickly run to our car, throw our cases in the boot, and get in and drive off! Drive off fast!"

"Car? But our car…"

"…It's parked at the front!" Randhira smiled in eagerness.

"The police found it?"

"No! Porush and Satto Bibi hid it."

"Why would they do that?"

"I said I'd tell you when we get back."

Sunil gave a bewildered glance at Randhira.

"Okay. In short. I used to go out with Porush's brother, Aaroush, during university. We broke up after a year. After breaking up with me, they married him to a girl from the village. Despite having had two children with this woman, he still loved me, and the grief of losing me eventually killed him."

"Is that true?"

"Absolutely. Now, thinking that I am responsible for the death of Porush's brother, they set a trap for us. Ajay is Ajay Pranjpe! He and his fucking bitch wife, Manisha Pranjpe, helped them do this to us!"

"Ah yes, Ajay Pranjpe from Pranjpe Steels and Electronics? Why does he need to do this? He is so busy that he cannot drop everything and come and help Porush trap us."

"That's what I asked. Listen to this. Aaroush, Porush's brother, and Ajay knew each other from university, and Ajay owed him a favor."

"I see. But Ajay Pranjpe?"

"I was shocked as well. But hasn't your father invested…"

"...Yes! I know!" screamed Randhira under her breath.

"What do they want from us? Why do they want us to marry?"

"This is the one that made my jaw drop. They want us to get married and take care of Aaroush's children. One child is disabled." She held back her selfish undertone, intentionally lying, and wanting her freedom.

"What? Why us? Just because you went out with him, and he couldn't handle a break and ended up dying. Why should we take care of his children? They should put them up for adoption. What of Aaroush's wife?"

"After Aaroush died, his wife died, and so did his parents."

"Ouch! That's very sad."

"Yes, we cannot go around adopting children of our ex-girlfriends or ex-boyfriends, now, can we?"

"Can't Porush or Satto Bibi take care of them? We can give them money to support them."

"Both Satto and her husband are dying. They haven't got long."

"Porush?"

"He cannot support them."

"We can give him money."

"Why should we?"

"What of the lion?"

"He is a pet."

"A pet?! Who the fuck has a lion as a pet?"

Randhira scrunched her eyes. "Please! I know many billionaires with pet cheetahs and other big cats."

Sunil shrugged his shoulders. "Yeah!"

"Renu? Can I ask you something?"

"Quickly, we need to pack."

"These children…they aren't yours, are they?"

"Are you mad, Sunil? Do I look old enough to be their mother?"

"May not look it, but you are old enough to be their mother."

"Sunil, if you have trust issues, I don't think our relationship will last long. They are not my children. Period. Now, it's up to you to believe me or not. But I need to get the fuck out of here. You can sit here and give them money and offer you support. I am not."

Sunil did not have an answer.

"Sunil, don't overthink. I am telling you the truth."

"It doesn't make any sense. Why would they do that… that girl looks rather like you."

"Fine, Sunil. Believe whatever you want. Satto Bibi will come with our outfit in one hour. After she has left, I will pick up my bag and leave! You can stay if you like."

Again, Sunil did not know what else to say and gazed back at Randhira.

"I am not taking on the responsibility of someone else's children. Right now, we need to drive off. When we return, we will get married and then go abroad, where no one can find us and do this to us again."

"You will marry me?" Sunil said with expectant eyes. Randhira had now tugged on Sunil's heartstrings.

"Yes, but when we get back!"

"Why not we get married here and then run away? They are setting the altar, after all."

Randhira became hesitant and began to think of a decent way of refusing again.

"It will be tough; we might not be able to get out. And I don't want to marry like this. I want a destination wedding!"

"Abroad?" Sunil smiled excitedly, falling for the dreamy trap being set by Randhira.

"Yes!" Randhira hissed and smiled. "It'll be perfect. White sand, clear waters, blue sky, and all our relatives and friends!"

Sunil smiled and nodded, and they hugged.

"Just wait for the evening, and we shall make our move," whispered Randhira.

"What if the lion attacks?" Sunil wondered.

"We must take the risk and get in the car quickly. Once we are in the car, we are safe."

Sunil nodded hard and asked, "So we wait until Satto Bibi sends up my things and the wedding outfits?"

"Yes. We take the things when Satto Bibi brings them up for us and then pretend to get ready. In the evening, at the right moment, we sneak out and drive off back home." Randhira's intention spread like wildfire throughout her veins.

Chapter 8: Ameeran

R andhira and Sunil did not have to wait long for Satto Bibi to come to the Suite to hand them over their outfits. When she did so, not much exchange of words took place between her and Sunil and Randhira; however, she did tell them to come down in the evening and start getting ready for their wedding.

Randhira and Sunil had long, relaxing showers, knowing they'd not be wearing fresh clothes after the wash as they had not packed for their extended, unexpected stay at the Ateet. Nevertheless, they got ready not in the outfits given to them by Satto Bibi but in the set of clothes that smelt the least from their bags.

As the evening approached, Randhira's determination to escape grew stronger. She paced, sat, bit her nails, and took deep breaths, her mind focused on the escape plan. On the other hand, Sunil lay on the bed, his resolve unwavering, and eventually dozed off, ready for the impending challenge. The contrast in their actions heightened the tension of the impending escape.

As the evening descended into darkness, Randhira woke Sunil with a sense of urgency, gesturing for him to get up. The time for action had arrived, and they couldn't afford to waste a moment.

In the meantime, Satto Bibi, Porush, Ajay, and Binki were setting the altar and putting up decorations. They took time out to dress up and make sure everything looked great. They were unaware of the urgent and suspenseful escape plan in the Suite.

However, Sunil and Randhira's mission was to reach the car and drive off without being caught. Randhira cautiously opened the door, making sure not to make a sound. She didn't roll the bag along the carpeted floor. Still, she lifted it by the handle, stepping out slowly and scanning the corridor for any signs of danger. Every step they took was a risk, a step closer to potential discovery.

The old-fashioned corridor was lit well with wall lamps, and there was no noise. No noise came from Ameeran's room, either.

Randhira tiptoed on carrying her bag, and Sunil followed suit. Their first checkpoint was to make it quietly across the corridor and get to the door that said "Stairs," far from where the Suite and the lifts were—the opposite side. Randhira, followed by Sunil, snuck through, and made it up to Ameeran's room. The door was mostly shut, only a tiny gap. In her room, she was excited and packing away. It was a serene scene, starkly contrasting to the tense situation unfolding.

Randhira did not risk peaking in, yet slowly moved across and crept to the door that read, "Stairs." Sunil stealthy did the same.

The first frontier was reached. Next was to get downstairs without making a sound. Randhira opened the door. Fortunately for them, it did not make any sound, and they got through and closed it behind them. Slowly and softly, they began their descent downwards. It was many floors up, so it took a while. Still, they reached the bottom of the stairs without making too much noise and, most importantly, without bumping into anyone.

ATEET – THE PAST

Having gotten downstairs, Randhira again slowly opened the door, which opened out onto the lift area on the ground floor, and she popped her head out again. She saw no one in sight. Slightly out of breath, she went out, and Sunil followed. They tiptoed, keeping an eye out, and moved into the gallery. The gallery smelled dusty, and Randhira was trying not to react to the covered portraits of Aaroush and his deceased parents. She led the way across the large gallery into the library. They crossed the library cautiously in the same way. The library was cold, and the pungent smell of dust did not help. Sunil could taste the dust, too, but refrained from coughing to avoid making a sound. The library was cleared, and then there was the big room with the large door where Randhir was chained. But it was the fire exit they were interested in.

The naïve man, unbeknownst to his lover's past and the heartless mother of two, headed towards the fire exit. Randhira gently pressed down the discolored handled bar. Pushing it gently was not going to open the brutal, rusty door. Sunil took over and applied force, and the door opened with a sound. A considerably loud sound. Loud enough to reach the gallery. They looked around and found no one behind or could see in the distance.

Wasting no time, Randhira and Sunil exited via the fire escape door, believing no one had seen them. But little did they know, hot on their trail since Randhira walked out onto the area where the lifts were, there was someone behind them and followed him to see where they were going.

Randhira and Sunil, unaware they'd been seen, slowly moved across the entrance and started heading over to the vehicle parked further down the road, extremely close to the lake. Still carrying the cases and trying to make no clatter, the two treaded down to their car.

Unknown to this, Satto Bibi, Porush, Ajay, and Binki were dressed, and the altar was ready. Amidst this, Bansi strolled into the decorated room to Satto Bibi, Porush, Ajay, and Binki's surprise, chewing on something. He was half-dressed in his priest outfit. It appeared he was initially dressed but had removed the kurta and was wearing a vest and pajamas.

"You aren't ready? Go get ready in your priest outfit." Bibi's cheeks briefly turned crimson in frustration. "Renu and Sunil will be down in a moment now!"

"Hah!" Bansi chuckled and walked up slowly with his hands at his back, and he shook his head, mocking his wife.

"Ajay, Binki, go to the lifts area to see if they are there." Satto Bibi gestured his hand toward the lift.

"Hah!" Bansi laughed inwardly, which stopped Ajay and Binki in their footsteps.

"What is wrong with you? Go get ready." Satto Bibi's tone more demanding than a mere suggestion.

"For what?" Bansi again laughed.

"For *Bhabhi* and Sunil's wedding, Baba," Porush cleared up and moved closer to him.

"Hah! Bansi again giggled.

Bansi continued to chew on a betel leaf.

"What is it, Baba?" Porush's head tilted left.

"You're chewing betel leaf? Before the wedding?" Satto Bibi's clenched her jaw.

"They are leaving," Bansi said casually, continuing to walk around admiring the hard work everyone had put in.

The ground had slipped from beneath Satto Bibi's feet, whereas Porush had gotten blurred vision for a second or two. Ajay and Binki, still in their senses, ran up to Satto Bibi to hold her up because she would have fallen otherwise. Porush gathered himself and shook his head violently. Satto Bibi, Porush Ajay, and Binki did not believe their ears for a while and stood in shock and silence.

"No." Porush's eyes widened in astonishment.

"Yes," Bansi nodded with his back to everyone.

"Baba, this no time for jokes!"

"*Oye*! I don't even have time for stupid jokes. She is leaving as we speak. They must have started the car by now. I am going." Bansi started to leave through another door.

"She held Ameeran and promised her…" Satto Bibi said softly and unbelievingly.

Bansi stopped and turned to Satto Bibi. He violently flapped his hand at her, shunning away her comment, and left, leaving Satto Bibi humiliated. She was not offended by her husband but by the woman who had promised to take her children. Fury and anger raged inside the old, short woman.

She breathed fire and let herself loose from Ajay and Binki's gentle hold.

"Porush... Ajay... go now!" Satto Bibi commanded.

Porush and Ajay exchanged glances and dashed for the lobby to witness this with their own eyes. Binki and Satto Bibi marched behind the men in great rage. Porush ran outside; it was dark, and the wind was crisp but fresh. Ajay joined himself shortly. They looked here and prayed and hoped they would not see anyone there. But they did. They saw Randhira and Sunil put their cases in the boot.

"Hey!" Porush felt his blood boil.

Randhira and Sunil, both heard him. Sunil slammed down the boot as the cases were in. Sunil headed toward the driving seat, but Randhira ran over to the driver's side and pushed Sunil, gesturing him to go to the passenger side and sit in the passenger seat.

"Let me..."

"...No, Sunil! If you drive and someone gets in the way, you'll stop, but today, if anyone stands in my way... I will not!"

"Renu!" Sunil's words were barely audible.

"I'm driving! Quick! Get in!" Randhira ordered.

Sunil followed her command.

"I'm central locking the car! We leave straight away; otherwise, they will not let us leave," Randhira said starting the car.

"Hey!" Porush shouted.

"You don't have the heart to do that!" Sunil said.

"Watch me, Sunil! Today, I will run over anyone that gets in our way!" Sunil's lips formed an "O" in shock.

With Randhira in the driving seat and Sunil in the front passenger seat, Randhira pressed the power button. The car struggled to start, but eventually, it did. She pushed the pedal down and vigorously swung the steering wheel, swinging the entire car around as fast as she could to face in the direction of the exit gate. She drove the car forward and stopped when she saw Ajay and Porush running towards the car. Sunil was relieved.

"Renu, there is a gap, head towards that, don't harm them," Sunil advised. Randhira revved the engine as she saw the two men running towards and shouting at them.

"Does it look as though I give a damn!" Randhira answered and sped towards the men; Porush ran towards the car. The car, picking up speed, bulleted towards him. Ajay withdrew and moved to the side to make way for the vehicle, but Porush, adamant he was to stop them, continued. By this time, Satto Bibi and Binki were outside and about to witness a horrific collision.

Porush did not stop and continued to advance as did Randhira towards him.

"Stop Renu, you'll kill him!"

"Sunil! You are such a *Fattu!*"

Poush was not going to stop.

Satto Bibi's heart skipped a beat to see her only remaining grandchild run towards his possible death.

"Porush! No!" Satto Bibi's tone increased.

It appeared that no one was going to back out. Still, to everyone's surprise, Randhira hit the brakes hard, which took the possibility of any fatality out of any possible impact. Her hitting the brake threw Sunil and her forward, and both were in discomfort from the hard stop.

The car hit Porush despite the braking, and he flew in the air. His back hit the bonnet, his chest hit the windscreen, and he somersaulted. He hit the top, followed by the boot, and landed hard behind the car on the ground. The windscreen was partially damaged, and the vehicle was dented everywhere Porush's body had hit.

"Argh!" Porush let out a loud cry in pain. Porush lay there in pain, and Ajay went to his aid. The windscreen was damaged. Porush was severely grazed and bruised. Blood poured from Porush's wounds.

"Porush!" Satto Bibi shouted in concern. Binki gasped in distress.

Randhira, showing no remorse, hit the pedal, and headed towards the path and the exit gate.

For that, she needed to drive past the entrance of Ateet, where Satto Bibi and Binki stood.

Randhira's car was in motion again, but now the short, old, strong-willed woman stood in her way. She stood there, her hands out wide, blocking the car's path. Randhira stopped the car meters away from her. Randhira again revved the engine as she looked into Satto Bibi's fiery, piercing, and adamant eyes fixed upon Randhira. Randhira's cold-blooded eyes looked back. A slight grin appeared on Randhira's face, and she pressed the pedal. The car raced toward Satto Bibi, but she would not move.

"Satto Bibi! Move! She won't stop!" Binki called out to her.

With the car heading towards Satto Bibi, Randhira realized she would not budge and hit the brakes again, letting out a loud screech. This threw both her and Sunil forward violently again. The car stopped a millimeter from the woman, whose hands smelt of sandalwood.

The screech was so loud that Ameeran heard it in her room; she was excitedly packing away but stopped and ran towards the window where the sound came from. One of the room's windows opened to the front of the guesthouse. She opened it and saw her uncle wounded and grazed, with Ajay trying to lift him and her great-grandmother standing in front of the car with her hands outstretched out wide.

Randhira lowered the car window slightly.

"Get out of my way, you stupid old woman!" Shouted Randhira.

Ameeran did not realize who was in the driving seat, but she knew the voice of a woman who spoke rudely to her great-grandmother.

"They are your children, Renu! You would leave them?" Satto asked in a great rage.

"What?" Sunil asked Randhira, turning his head towards her.

"She's lying!" Randhira turned to Sunil convincingly and said softly before turning back to Satto Bibi to reply.

"They are not! Let me go! Get out of my way!"

Ameeran realized it was her mother in the car, denying that she and her brother were her children. Ameeran's heart sank into the ocean of despair. Her dream was shattered. She felt sick, and a foul poison-like taste developed in her mouth. Her heart began to beat fast. Tears burst from her eyes, but she did not make a weeping noise. She held them back and made a gagging noise. Her unbelieving eyes turned enraged. She bit her lips and clenched her jaws in anger and disbelief at her mother's betrayal. She turned around in ferocity and headed downstairs like a wounded tigress.

"I will run you over!" Randhira warned Satto Bibi.

"Do it! Satto Bibi replied to Randhira.

"Don't think I won't do it. I will!" Randhira again threatened.

"I know you will because you are a demoness, Randhira Bajaj!"

"After I've run you over, can you stop me?"

"You're right!" Satto Bibi put down her hands. "I cannot stop you...but he definitely can!" Satto moved out of the way of the car to both Randhira's and everyone else's amazement.

Elevating her voice as loud as she could, Satto Bibi cried out into the mountains, the hills, and the lake, "Aaroush!"

Within two to three seconds. The snarling could be heard, and a loud reply was heard in the form of a roar. The roar of the king of the jungle returned in response.

"Stop her!" Satto shouted again.

Another great roar followed.

"Randhira's eyes widened in fear, but her arrogance prevailed over all feelings and emotions. She closed the window and raced towards the gate in the BMW.

Within a moment, she saw the great cat in front galloping towards her, roaring, with its mouth open, jaws on show, and death in its eyes. The car and the lion were racing towards each other for a direct head-on collision. Sunil put his head back in terror, and his eyes amplified as he saw the predator race towards them.

Randhira could see the lion racing towards the driver's side. She gathered that if he pounced, he'd break the windscreen, and her beautiful, soft neck would be in her jaws.

Her quick, sharp thinking and tremendous driving skills had to come into action. She waited for the right moment, and as the lion leaped, she pulled up the handbrake and turned the steering wheel hard to the left to perform a complete 180-degree turn to face the opposite direction to the lion. Still, the lion's energy, adrenaline, emotions, and velocity were beyond expectation. After all, his lifelong friend had died because of this woman. The lion had no intention of letting this woman go, and as the car reached 90 degrees, the lion, with his jaws open as wide as possible, made an impact with the passenger's window, shattering the glass to pieces and entering the vehicle. The lion was half inside the car, half hung out, and had Sunil's entire head in its mouth, with its jaw locked tight around his neck. Blood spurted everywhere; Sunil's death cry was short as his vocal cords were cut, his breathing pipe was severed, and so nearly was his head. Blood went all over Randhira, and she cried out loud at Sunil's horrific and tragic death while performing the fast maneuver.

Even at the sheer speed of the turn, the lion managed to hang on. It half hung from the car because its mouth had locked Sunil's entire head in, and when the vehicle did complete the whole 180 degrees turn, the sudden brake jerked the lion off the car along with Sunil's head in its mouth and threw him at a considerable distance from the vehicle.

"Argh!" Randhira screamed in horror at Sunil's lifeless and bloody body. But she had no time to react. She was facing the wrong way, and the lion was not far away.

She saw the lion throwing out Sunil's head from his mouth, snarling and roaring.

In shock and covered in Sunil's blood, she saw the decapitated body sitting beside her, erupting, and spurting out blood from the neck, where the head was severed off completely. She saw the passenger side window completely smashed and the windscreen half shattered, broken, and damaged.

"Argh!" she screamed but was quick to react and, with great courage, leaned across the dead body of Sunil, who still sat beside her, opened the passenger door, and unclipped the seat belt. As she unclipped the seat belt, her body fell towards her.

"Argh!" Randhira let out another shriek and pushed the dead body of her love away from her with great force. Eventually, the body fell out of the car completely, and she leaned across to close the dented door.

The body's legs got stuck in between the door and the car, but another big, vigorous shove helped get the body completely out of the vehicle. She pulled the door shut with a great bang.

By then, the lion had galloped close to the passenger's side. Randhira again outwitted the animal with excellent maneuvering and started the car. She reversed fast, looking backwards, and performed a perfect J turn to face the front and away from Ateet, the lion, and Satto Bibi. She pressed the pedal hard, the car wheel spun, the exhaust let out an unexpected large bang and sparks, and the car raced towards the gate.

The lion saw this and let out a great roar at Randhira and the car. Angry to have not gotten Randhira and the wrong person, the lion gave chase at full speed again.

Seeing death gaining up on her in the rearview mirror, which luckily was intact, she continued to accelerate and stepped on the accelerator pedal, speeding toward the gate.

"Over my dead body, you fucking bastards!" She shouted, and she raced away from the giant cat.

The cat was gaining speed over the car, and realizing this, the cat raced closer and sprung itself in the air and latched its sharp paws onto the bonnet and his teeth on the back windscreen shattering it to pieces, and the cat's mouth was inches away from the back of Randhira's head. Randhira's quick thinking came into play as the path turned onto the main road. With her perfect maneuvering, she threw the BMW into the turn, around the corner, and onto the main road. This sudden turn threw the feline off the vehicle quickly and smashed the great king cat's body against big rocks at the turn. The hard turn put the car onto two wheels and then on the other two until it stabilized on four and sped away onto the main road.

"Woohoo! Ya!" Randhira shouted victoriously.

The lion lay in shock and defeated on its side. The lion's scars and scrapes from the impact did not seem severe, but how it smashed against the rugged rocks ascertained that internal damage was imminent from the ever-so-hard clash with the rocks. Despite much disdain from the collision, the lion rose, growled, and then roared. He made a final attempt to give chase, but the grave internal damage meant he had no more energy. The impact was severe when he crashed against the rocks. The brave cat sat down, licked its wounds, hung its tongue out, and glanced in the distance at the car as it got further and further out of its sight.

"Aaroush!" Porush limped up to the feline. It had its head on the ground, and the breathing was becoming irregular. The lion closed its eyes, and tears rolled down Porush's eyes.

Ajay ran up to the gate with Binki, with Satto Bibi not far behind. Porush's leg was bleeding profusely. He limped and went and stood beside Ajay and Binki. Satto Bibi hastily caught up and stood behind the defeated lion, who lay on the ground, with life fleeing from its body gradually.

"Aaroush?"

Porush looked at her with wet eyes and shook his head. Satto Bibi's eyes became numb. She took a deep breath. Her heart cursed Randhira. They all stood there, watching the car go further away.

A fifth person gently pushed its way through the four. It was Ameeran as she looked upon the car driving away with the false promises and her dreams. She tightened her lip angrily and stared without blinking. The mother's deception had left her furious, and her eyes turned red.

She lowered her head and gazed at the ground angrily, as did the others.

She had gotten away. Randhira blew a strand of hair from her face as she kept her hands tight on the wheel. She looked back at the broken screen and then at the dented passenger door. She, too, was grazed and bruised from all the shattered pieces that flew all around her. Blood, however, was everywhere in the car. She continued to look ahead and drive.

"Yes!" she screamed victoriously. She knew it was a close call. She wiped her nose with the back of her dirty hand and let out a short snuffle. She shed a tear or two for Sunil but then gathered herself as she came to terms with the fact that he was gone and that she had escaped the trap set for her.

She didn't take her foot off the pedal until she knew she was far from Ateet. Until then, she threw the BMW into sharp corners, which the vehicle handled well.

Suddenly, she heard the ring of her mobile telephone in her pocket. She reached out and saw she had a signal, and the call was from an unknown number. Although thrilled to have gotten a signal, she was surprised and wondered who was ringing her. She answered the phone,

"Hello," Randhira answered.

"After all, you deceived us again, like before, *Bhabhi*." It was Porush. He had the phone on speakerphone mode. Satto Bibi, Binki, Ajay, and Ameeran stood around the mobile telephone, still at the gate.

"Fuck you all. You all can go to hell after what you did to me!" Randhira screamed back.

"Sunil's body lies here."

"A lion attacked us when we left the guesthouse! I will tell everyone when I get back. They will come and collect Sunil's body. I suggest you all get the fuck out of there before the police comes. Porush, you take your family and that lion to your village. If anyone asks you, you don't know anything. Ajay and Binki clean up the place, lock it and get the fuck out of there. This is our story! It is best for everyone."

"Aaroush, the lion, he's dead," Porush informed.

"Good!"

"You are so heartless!" Satto Bibi shouted.

"It tried to kill me!"

"We all need to do what's in our best interests?" Ajay intervened.

"Ajay Pranjpe and Manisha Pranjpe, with the help of a few locals, conspired to trap and kill Sunil Grewal and Randhira Bajaj! Now, this headline is not good for anyone!" Randhira explained.

Everyone looked at one another in disgruntlement.

"Sunil's death was an accident." Ajay's eyes diverted to the ground. "No one intended for that to happen."

"Oh, just shut up, will you, Ajay! Stop talking about the past. Think ahead. Think of your project. And for your kind information, even if no one wanted Sunil to die, he died. Porush and Satto Bibi could have stopped the lion if they wanted to! We all know that. Instead, the lion was called upon to attack us. Be grateful! I am doing you all a favor."

"Favor? Or striking a deal?" Asked Binki.

"Call whatever you want bitch! Here is the deal. My end of the bargain is I won't name and shame you. Your end of the bargain is you all keep away from me and keep your mouths shut. You get to stay out of jail, and I get to keep my freedom."

"What will you say if anyone asks where you stayed for the past few days?" Ajay asked.

"We'll say we booked what seemed to be a guesthouse. We got there, and no one was there. The guesthouse was locked and abandoned, so we parked by the lake and slept in the car; the following morning, the car wasn't working, so we got stuck. Sunil finally managed to fix the car in a day or two, and as we were about to leave, we encountered a lion. Tell your IT geek to wipe any trace that could lead to any of us. You can say he was testing out the new booking site. Say it was meant to be offline, but he put it live or online for testing purposes and managed to get a freak booking, which happened to be ours. Tell him to clear up the stuff about you jamming signals, etc. Get your zookeepers and lion tammers out! Nothing should lead to any of you or me!"

"Do you know ASP Mohan Varma?" Asked Binki.

"I do; he is an exemplary cop! In fact, we... forget it!

"Oh my gosh!" Binki said. "You and him, huh?"

"Why? Was he not on your list? Or the track record you had for me, huh?" Randhira mocked. "There is more to me than meets the eye, bitch!"

Binki and Ajay looked at one another.

"Stop calling me bitch, you callous woman!" Binki shouted. "ASP Mohan Varma will not let this go lightly, neither will Sunil's family! They will want an investigation."

"And they will find nothing," Randhira answered.

181

"The love of your life just died…" Binki continued.

"…Bitch Binki… you tidy up everything up. I have the upper hand now that Sunil's head is rolling on the ground!"

"What do you want?" Ajay interjected.

"Stupid Ajay…as I said, let's go with this story!"

Binki tensed her jaws, but Ajay stopped her from swearing back.

"Now, stupid Ajay and bitch Binki, move your asses and start tidying up everything. Clear everything. Lock up everything. And fuck off back to your home! You know nothing of this! If you want to stay out of trouble and want your project to succeed or even materialize, you cannot be associated with Sunil's death. No one will invest with you if they find out you were involved in the murder of Sunil Grewal!"

"Why do this, Randhira?" Binki said. "Just take responsibility for your kids. Just come back and take them with you; look after them."

"Take responsibility for what, you bitch? This is my life! I choose what I want to do, not anyone else. Not even God himself. And why am I doing this?

For my freedom! I don't want to be a mother to teenagers at thirty-six! As for you, Porush, take your family and that lion, if he's still alive, back to your village and forget this ever happened and forget about me!"

Everyone remained quiet.

"I will get everything cleaned up and cleared out from here; give me some time," Ajay said.

"Fuck you, Ajay Pranjpe. The moment I get back to the capital city, I am going to the police, and then they will come out here to pick up Sunil's body. You have hours."

Ajay and Binki exchanged worried looks and headed back inside to make phone calls and arrangements. Leaving Porush, Satto Bibi, and Ameeran standing there in the cold.

"I haven't met someone so selfish and heartless as you, *Bhabhi*. This is your family," said Porush.

"Firstly, cut out the *Bhabhi* crap! I am not your *Bhabhi*! Secondly, this is not my family; it's yours, so you take care of it. And finally, you have met someone as selfish and heartless as me. My freedom and my life come first. Before anything and anyone!" The previous day flashed before her, impounding her frustration.

"Even before your children?" Ameeran asked in her weeping yet angry, soft voice.

Randhira remained quiet after hearing the soft, livid voice. Randhira took a deep breath and calmly spoke to her, "*Bachcha*... go live with your uncle. It's best for everyone."

"Then why did you say what you said?" Ameeran insisted as a child.

"Forget all that I said, *bachcha*. You are grown up now. Do as I say."

"Don't call me *bachcha*!" Ameeran shouted as she wept. "My mother gave me that name, whom I only saw and met for thirty minutes in that room. My name is Ameeran."

"Then listen, Ameeran. Forget about me. Look after your brother, grandparents, and uncle, and study hard for a good life. Forget about the past. Forget about the Ateet."

"And you? Will you forget the fact you have two children?"

"Forget about me, Ameeran! It was all in the past."

Satto Bibi stepped in, "And the past always has a way of returning! You haven't seen the last of us!"

"You are now threatening me? What will you do? Come after me?" You all will never find me!" That I assure you! And even if you did find me, what would you do? Kill me? Hah! You cannot!"

"You can go hide in any corner of the world, and I will find you…Ms Randhira Bajaj!" Ameeran spoke with a stern, angry, and disappointed voice.

"Oh, is it so? Then let me tell you something, *bachcha*, I don't take threats very well. I am not the conventional mother whose heart will melt at the sight of her children. Don't get in the way of me and my life."

"As Bibi said, this is not the end! I am coming for you Ms Randhira Bajaj! I am coming for you!

"I'd like to see that, *bachcha*!"

"Even I would like to see that, Renu!" Satto Bibi shouted.

"Leave it, Satto Bibi; Porush told me you don't have long!"

"I won't die until you have been taught a lesson."

"Then you and Ameeran better hurry up!"

"Oh, we shall!" Ameeran broke in, holding her great-grandmother's hand tightly. "Bibi is going nowhere. We are coming for you!"

"I like it, *bachcha*. I… Like it. Just out of interest, let's say you found me. What would you do?"

"What do I do to you when I find you? Well, let's keep that a surprise, shall we?"

"I am always up for a challenge, *bachcha*, but don't forget if a snake goes hungry for a long time, it doesn't hesitate to devour its eggs or children!"

"Be it snake or lioness, the same blood runs in our veins. My appearance, attitude, anger, endurance, and tendencies are the same as yours. From this day onwards, Ms Randhira Bajaj, you will always be second checking and looking over your shoulder again to see if I'm there."

"Is that so, *bachcha*?"

"Yes, that is so. Believe it or not… one day, you'll look over your shoulder, and I shall be standing there, looking straight at you in your eyes. You will have no problem recognizing me…because I look exactly like you… *Maa*! I am calling you this for the first and last time ever."

"In that case, I await your next move," Randhira challenged.

"Hold on in there tight; I am coming for you!" Ameeran accepted.

About the Author

Raj Bansal was born in Southampton, Hampshire, and currently resides with his wife in Ashford, Middlesex. He is an IT consultant by profession, but writing is his passion. Thank you for reading his book. If you enjoyed it, please take a moment to leave a review at your favorite retailer.

Other Books by Raj Bansal

Landsfor, Discoveries and Revelations – Book 1

A fast-paced YA fantasy novel packed with dark secrets and mystical forbidden realms!

No family, friend, or foe is free from suspicion amidst the palace intrigue, and Dymondo is faced with the challenge of determining whom he can trust.

Dymondo's investigation leads him down a precarious path of conflicting emotions and an enthralling journey into a forbidden jungle where he discovers a dark truth about his family and the secret of his birth.

Will Dymondo be able to solve the mystery?

Order your copy and join Dymondo in his biggest quest yet!

Landsfor, Frozenfire (Landsfor Series Book 2)

All is well in the Kingdom of Gammafor and Fourtfor as Dymondo Rain the islands' just, capable and righteous leader comes into his own as King with his new beloved Queen by his side.

Dymondo is haunted by nightmares from his youth and a strange intruder has come to the gate of his Kingdom to announce unwanted news. Dymondo aims to run his two islands with responsibility and pride, ensuring peace and prosperity for his people, but now his Kingdom is under threat from Dymondo's most feared adversary, his older brother, Shilathaar.

On his own island of Forprimiera, Shilathaar Rain has begun to build a vast army threatening to overthrow anyone that stands in his way of seizing control of all four islands of the Kingdom of Landsfor.

Shilathaar is strong, cruel, and imprudent, and his aggressive collecting of allies presents a palpable threat to the realm.

Dymondo is left with no choice. He must protect his Kingdom from the approaching great war. But he is far from ready.

If he wishes to defeat his enemies, Dymondo must battle his own insecurities, fears and shortcomings, strengthen his armies, gain allies and go on a dangerous quest to recover a divine ancient weapon.

If he fails, he and his kingdom will perish under the approaching inferno of war. With the help of his trusted companions, Dymondo must voyage to other lands, explore secret chambers and venture into dangerous caverns, battling any hindrances that may arise in his path.

Only then can he gain the great power of the Frozenfire and, in the process, discover himself.

Will Dymondo emerge victorious and successful in achieving his goals? Order your copy now and join Dymondo's quest for more than just a victory!

Raj Bansal